Daniel Pembrey

Daniel Pembrey grew up in Nottinghamshire beside Sherwood Forest. He studied history at Edinburgh University and received an MBA from INSEAD business school. Daniel then worked for ten years at a large, Seattle-based Internet company – most recently in Luxembourg.

He now writes thrillers and psychological suspense stories, and occasionally contributes non-fiction articles to publications including *The Times*. You can follow him on Facebook, *facebook.com/DPembrey* and Twitter, *@DPemb*. To receive occasional updates and offers of free exclusive content, please sign up at *danielpembrey.com*.

Praise for Daniel Pembrey

Daniel Pembrey tells a cracking tale with verve and style. He can write, the jury's not out on that one ...
Susan Hill, *Booker Prize short-listed author*

Praise for *The Candidate*

A very readable Euro thriller with a strong sense of setting. This is well worth a read, and has shades of Elmore Leonard and other hard-boiled American detective writers. But it's also up to date, with an insight into modern Euro-crime which is all too accurate.
Katharine Quarmby, *award-winning writer, TV producer and journalist*

Daniel Pembrey has an intelligent and subtle style that moves us along quietly in the development of the mystery. It is to his credit that this novella has a very realistic scenario ...
Marvin Vernon, *Cool and Blue Reviews*

Pembrey provides grit, heat and intrigue with a European flare with this well-written tale of intrigue. He writes with a crisp attitude as he keeps the tension high while slowing unraveling each twist with perfect timing.
Dianne Bylo, *Amazon Top 500 Reviewer*

This short read is fast paced, and keeps you wondering what will happen next. Nick is a sympathetic character, so you can't help but root for him to solve the mystery of who was in his bed.

Nancy Famolari, *Amazon Vice Voice*

Pembrey is writing about places and jobs where he has worked, just as he did in 'The Woman Who Stopped Traffic', which is set in California. With his flair for realism and insider knowledge he doesn't just push the door open, he throws it wide to reveal the good, the bad and the dangerous.

Clare O'Beara, *Amazon Top 1000 Reviewer,*
Winner of the Arkady Renko Short Story Contest 2014
judged by Martin Cruz Smith

Pembrey has created an engaging main character in Nick Thorneycroft, and he's placed him in a potentially very dangerous situation. I enjoyed reading how Nick tried to do his job and at the same time piece together clues as to what happened during his blackout. This is a man who suddenly finds himself completely out of his depth, and we get to see how he deals with it.

Cathy Cole, *Amazon Vine Voice and Top 1000 Reviewer*

It packs an awful lot in, all of it exciting, and Daniel Pembrey manages to keep the various strands separate enough that it doesn't fall into confusion. The ending is perfect for a novella . . .

Cleo Bannister, *Cleopatra Loves Books*

Also by Daniel Pembrey

The Harbour Master

The Woman Who Stopped Traffic

Simon Sixsmith: A Ghost Story

THE CANDIDATE

A LUXEMBOURG THRILLER

DANIEL PEMBREY

www.danielpembrey.com

Copyright © 2013, Daniel Pembrey.

All rights reserved.
No part of this book may be reproduced, lent or
otherwise distributed in any form without permission.
Please do not participate in or encourage piracy
of copyrighted material in violation
of authors' rights.

This is a work of fiction. Names, characters,
places and incidents are either the products of
the author's imagination or are used fictitiously,
and resemblance to actual persons living or dead,
businesses, companies, events or locales
is coincidental.

ISBN: 978-1-4996-7047-9

Jacket design by Patrick Savile

Typeset in ITC Legacy Serif by Ellipsis Digital Limited, Glasgow.

Contents

The Morning After	1
There She Is	12
Xanant	21
The Loop	28
Just Lunch	38
Debriefed	48
The Offer	58
Where Now?	68
Pfaffenthal	77
Room 550	86
Luxembourg's Landlord	97
Ducal Casino	104
The Bridge	111
Coda	124

The Morning After

They were black, croissant-shaped and instantly recognisable to my male brain. Still, it took me a few seconds to comprehend the scrunched-up pair of women's underwear on the floor of my dim Luxembourg apartment. The effects of some spirit, vodka possibly, clouded my vision.

I crouched down and picked them up. My fingers were shaky and I felt sweat on the back of my neck – even though it was the depths of winter. Whose were they? I scanned the rest of my bedroom for clues. The parquet floor and high ceiling swam murkily; it was too dark to see much with the shutters closed, and my fierce hangover wasn't helping. Yet all the other clothes strewn around looked to be my own. There were my Hugo Boss black trousers, my metallic-grey work shirt, my belt and leather slip-ons. Somewhere there too, hopefully, was my old Rolex.

I couldn't see the bed properly. There was no one in it, but I couldn't tell whether there was a depression in the mattress from someone else having slept there.

In my trouser pocket I found my phone, the battery almost dead, Claire asking after midnight: *Can we talk?* Again. The last text was from Phil at 3.17 a.m: *Wher r u?*

I needed to see what else was in my pockets. Credit-card receipts? A woman's phone number?

There was a receipt from Ducal Casino for a bottle of Lanson champagne and two club sandwiches totalling 185 euros. It was time-stamped 02.44.

Nothing else.

I almost called Phil, but his text suggested that he didn't know the answer to my question either: where was I last night?

I winced as I opened the shutters and the window. Pigeons cooed from the stone balcony, which was dusted with snow. Didn't these creatures feel the cold? There was a mewling sound, a cat perhaps. Buses and other traffic rumbled along Avenue de la Liberté below. Opposite were old stone apartment buildings, low-rise but grandly so. I was naked, but I doubted anyone was looking in.

I turned around and the bedroom glared at me, the sheets and pillows blue-white. On the left side of the bed (the side I didn't sleep on) were a couple of blonde hairs, which caught the light like filigree. Those would be Claire's. She'd visited from London a week or so ago. We'd tried to work things out, declared defeat and then had break-up sex – the best sex of our relationship. I thought for a second the underwear might be hers, only why would they have suddenly appeared at the foot of my bed? The ghost of relationships past? Besides, they didn't look like Claire's. In some way that I couldn't quite identify, they weren't her style. Too . . . *foreign*-looking.

Well, they definitely weren't mine. And yet I was now their custodian. A far cry from a glass slipper, granted. I shook my head at the comparison, wincing at the pain this movement caused and hoping to God that I had some dispersible aspirin left in the bathroom cabinet.

I picked up the knickers again: there was no label, no La Perla, nothing. The material was soft and worn, and not showy – suggesting that their owner may not have been expecting to get naked. Which was something. At least they weren't an escort's.

Escorts were not my thing, but this wasn't the case for other professionals based here. Luxembourg was a city of just 100,000 people, teeming with overpaid ex-pats like myself. Many of the other foreigners were married, with families in other countries. The love nests they tended to share with weekday companions lay empty here at weekends, and particularly in this part of town, close to the financial centre. High-end escorts and mistresses kept the tills of Cartier and Gucci discreetly ringing just a few streets away.

At this precise moment – 9.17 on a Sunday morning, the red LED of my bedside clock announced – nothing could be ruled out.

I scrunched the knickers back up, about to throw them away – which felt wrong (after all, I must have had sex with whoever had been wearing them, or at least tried to), but the idea of stuffing them into a drawer seemed equally inappropriate.

I padded through to the bathroom and opened the mirrored cabinet door. No aspirin. Fuck. Madame Doriot, my landlady, might have picked some up on her weekly shop.

Then I noticed that my Gillette razor and shaving cream were more neatly arranged than usual. I'm not a slob, don't get me wrong, but the early morning rush often causes me to hurl them back into the cabinet (there's no space around the basin to leave them out).

I closed the cabinet and took in my reflection. Even with this hangover, time had been kind to me. I had laughter lines, but no grey hairs – and dark stubble to match. My clear, grey eyes had won me more compliments than I'd doubtless deserved – though they wouldn't today, bloodshot as they were. And maybe it was the rowing at university, maybe my dad coming from a line of steelworkers, but my shoulders, chest and abs had stayed in remarkably good condition without too much gym time.

At the age of thirty-five, I'd seen my fair share of benders – the usual Baltic stag weekends, university binges back in the day – but I'd never suffered memory loss like this before. Perhaps that's what it meant, arriving at the midpoint of life. A mental change as much as a physical one. Whatever I'd done last night, my head was telling me I was getting too old for it.

Then I noticed my neck: there appeared to be a love bite. I peered closer and saw that it *wasn't* a thousand capillaries that had burst beneath the skin; rather, it resembled a faint burning of the skin surface itself. But pale, almost imperceptible. Possibly my collar rubbing against the skin there? I was thinking about what else it could be when a key turned in the main door and it rattled open.

'Nicolas!'

Mme Doriot entered the little hallway beside the bathroom, staring open-mouthed.

'Christ,' I said, angrily grabbing a towel.

To everyone else I was Nick. To Mme Doriot, *Nicolas*.

'*Il faut frapper à la porte!*' I tried to assert. My attempt at French made me feel more vulnerable still. 'Please don't walk in here unannounced!'

She stood, looking po-faced. Her cheeks were caked with cracking foundation; her hair was dyed jet black. Mme Doriot was everything you'd expect of a French landlady, yet with something of the exotic about her, like a flower that had been left for too long in a hothouse. Her eyelashes fluttered like insect wings.

'My dog . . .' she began, then her eyes settled on the knickers. Not knowing what else to do with them, I'd let them fall at my bedroom door.

'Madame Doriot,' I said, walking out of the bathroom and kicking them away, 'I'd like to review the key situation here – whether I shouldn't have all the sets. You can't just barge in here like this!'

'I need to drop off these,' she said indignantly, holding up a string bag. It contained a litre of orange juice, some groceries and, if I wasn't mistaken, a pack of aspirin. 'I heard you come in late. You woke Monsieur Doriot.'

'We were loud?'

Who was *we*?

'My mind is elsewhere,' Mme Doriot changed her tune, reaching for a hall chair to sit down in, the contents of the string bag clinking on the wooden floor, 'ever since Mischa vanished.'

'Mischa?'

'My dog!'

Oh yes, of course, her yappy dog. 'Gone where?'

'I do not know.'

We were standing around the kitchen table of the Doriots' cramped apartment on the ground floor, behind the concierge office that Mme Doriot managed. M. Doriot had joined us, still in his striped pyjamas, eyes hooded. Once, he'd been a pharmacist, he'd told me – he'd owned a dispensary just down the street. It was now the ground floor of a private equity office.

I'd gone downstairs to ask for the other set of keys to my apartment. After the unknown events of last night, it felt important that people weren't able to just come and go. My position at the company I worked for was an important one; I handled highly sensitive information, often contained in documents that I brought home at night. Thankfully, not the previous night. Still, I needed to take precautions. I was playing in the big leagues now.

But something told me I wasn't going to get my hands on the other set of keys.

'Not enough sleep,' M. Doriot was complaining.

I nodded guiltily, my late return surely having been the cause.

'For me neither!' snapped Mme Doriot, dragging a heavy old phone onto the table. '*Il faut appeler . . .*' and then she said something fast in French, which mostly eluded me; something about having to phone someone about the dog, I believe.

'I could go out and look for it if you like,' I offered. I needed to go into the office anyway.

Mme Doriot ignored me and rounded on her husband with more fast French, the gist of her vent being, I'm pretty sure, that *he* should be the one out looking for the dog –

'*Je n'ai pas dormi!*' he cried, with beseeching hand gestures. He hadn't slept.

'*Et alors!*'

'I'm sorry for waking you,' I told him.

'I can't blame you.' He sighed and waved me away.

'Oh?' Had he seen her?

He winked at me in an avuncular way.

'Did you see us come in together?' I asked him.

'From behind,' he said, 'on the stair.' And he gave me a complicit smile.

I wanted to ask him more about my mystery companion, but Mme Doriot was huffing. She was still fighting with the phone, preoccupied with her missing dog.

'When did you last see Mischa?' I turned to her.

'Yesterday evening, when we came in from our walk. Mischa ran up the stairs and I tried to catch her, but – *hélas*.' She sighed.

'But there are only apartments up the stairs,' I puzzled. 'Where could she have gone?'

'Exactly!' Mme Doriot seized on my words. 'One of the *locataires* must have opened the door to her and stolen her. I am calling the police!'

'Don't do that,' I said.

Mme Doriot looked sharply at me. 'Why not?' she said, as though I had something to confess.

'Because there's also a door up to the attic, isn't there? The Australians on the second floor have been using it for storage. They may have left the door open.'

Mme Doriot's eyes held mine as she considered my hypothesis.

'It is possible,' she conceded, quickly pushing herself up from her chair, bracing her plump forearms against the wooden table surface.

I left Mme and M. Doriot on the ground floor waiting for the bewilderingly slow lift, M. Doriot having pulled a hunting jacket on over his pyjamas. I took the polished wooden stairs two at a time, as purposefully as my still-throbbing head would allow.

Opposite my apartment was the door to the attic. I pushed it open. A narrow set of steps led up to a high storage area. Climbing them, I could feel a cold draught. Dim light entered from outside, but it was blocked by stacked cardboard boxes belonging to the Australians.

I abandoned that idea and entered the front door of my place, going to the bedroom window, which I opened fully.

'Mischa!'

The cooing pigeons scattered, leaving the traffic noise below. And the mewling sound. More like a whining, in fact . . .

'*Mischa!*'

I clambered out onto the wall-head gutter. I was wearing a polo neck, thick jeans and Caterpillar boots, but the ice on the lead surfaces stung my fingers and palms, and my knees too, through the soon-damp denim. Crawling along, I tried not to look down to the street below, afraid that I might suddenly become unbalanced thanks to my lingering hangover.

Keeping my vision firmly on the horizontal, I glanced over at the apartment buildings opposite. I couldn't see any signs of life, but the locals tended to be secretive and security conscious; a man spotted crawling along a parapet would arouse suspicion.

The sky was anvil grey. Snowflakes drifted down. I could hear the faint sound of a TV in a neighbouring apartment: a sit-com or some game show, judging by the unnatural bursts of applause.

The whining became louder. I inched my way forward, my hands now numb, pressing into frozen, brittle leaves and pigeon shit. Beside a frosted dormer window, entangled in a cable, was a small, shivering white form.

Mischa glistened. Little icicles hung from the wet strands of her coat. Her eyes were faraway, almost lifeless, her head canted resignedly.

As soon as I got close enough, I untangled her rigid hind legs from the cable. Once released, they pedalled slowly from previous frustration. I cradled her trembling body to my neck; I could barely detect the warmth of her vital organs.

It struck me that, despite the cold, she was probably

dehydrated. I scooped up some snow from the top of the dormer roof and waited for it to melt in my cupped palm, before offering it to her little snout. Hesitantly, her sharp tongue licked at it.

That's when I noticed the skylight open on the roof – the area corresponding to the attic where the Australians kept their stuff.

'So that *is* how you got up here,' I chided Mischa gently, taking off my polo neck and wrapping it around her. In only my thin T-shirt I felt my ribcage contract from the cold. I pressed the dog against my shoulder with one hand and began to crawl carefully back to my place. Of course, Mme Doriot had let herself in to my apartment, and was waiting there with M. Doriot.

'Oh, *mon dieu*!' She grabbed Mischa from me, clasping the dog to her bosom. The dog was whimpering again. Mme Doriot's eyes were closed; she looked like she'd died and gone to heaven. 'Mischa,' she kept repeating, rubbing the little beast back to warmth.

M. Doriot looked on. And then at me: '*Mais qu'est-ce que c'est que ça?*' he said, gesturing at my neck.

Without my polo neck on, the splotch was visible.

'It's nothing,' I said.

He came closer, peering at it from under his hooded eyes. 'What medication is this?'

'What do you mean?'

'This is a topical treatment.'

'I don't know. I haven't used anything!'

'Maybe I am mistaken then,' M. Doriot said.

But something told me that his sharp eyes hadn't been deceived.

Had someone medicated me? And if so, what else had they done?

There She Is

Walking briskly in my thick jacket, I crossed the landmark Adolphe Bridge, swigging orange juice until the carton was empty. It was still snowing, cars hissing across the bridge in the slush. The fresh snow lay on the pavement, muffling my footsteps. The 'Snow Globe', was how some ex-pats referred to Luxembourg.

I stopped on the middle of the bridge – at the deepest point of the gulley. A low stone wall jutted out in places to create observation points. A couple of hundred feet below, the icy Pétrusse river surged along past the foot of Luxembourg Castle, into the Alzette and alongside our office in the Ville Basse. Where was my security pass?

I set down the empty carton of juice against the wall. The jacket I had on was the one I wore to work, but I couldn't find the credit-card-sized pass in any of the pockets. The reception desk would be unstaffed on a Sunday; there would be no one to let me in.

I began to get a sick feeling in my stomach as I thought about having to report the security breach caused by my lost pass. Our company provided payment-processing systems to banks and other such organisations: lots of proprietary know-how and sensitive customer data, our leadership team kept telling us. God knows why Claire had thought this would be my kind of gig, when I'd worked previously as a temp recruiter, and a sportswriter before that. She'd been working for an executive search firm at the time and had helped me make the leap.

But I couldn't blame Claire for me being behind with my recruiting targets while I was still in my six-month probationary period. I was potentially easy pickings for the rounds of cost-cutting that accompanied all the hiring our company was doing as it grew.

Hurriedly I patted myself down, drawing attention from passers-by. But the pass definitely wasn't where I usually kept it. Then I felt something below the side pocket. Something small and oblong-shaped, lodged in the hem. I checked my inside pocket again and found a hole in the stitching. My security pass had fallen down inside the lining and got stuck there.

I exhaled hard with relief; my breath was like white smoke in the cold air.

Snatching my phone out of my pocket, I tried to get hold of Phil. He wasn't answering. I started walking, passed Cartier and Gucci and soon found myself on Place d'Armes, with its bright carousel. Christmas excitement was in the air, kids squealing, the scent of melting chocolate wafting from the street vendors. My phone lit up.

'Phil!'

'Yeah.'

Phil was one of the technical gurus at the company. He was a programme manager, or perhaps a project manager; I was never quite sure what he did. The few times he'd tried to explain his job to me it had gone straight over my head. We'd met at work soon after I'd arrived and had fast become regulars at Luxembourg's only English pub.

'What happened last night?' I asked.

'I was going to ask you the same thing.' His Estuary English accent sounded whiny, as if he was complaining.

'I don't remember . . . I guess we went to the casino?' I remembered the receipt for the Lanson and two club sandwiches.

'Not me. I looked for you in Zin Zen. The barmaid said you'd scored and left.'

'We were in Zin Zen?'

He laughed, slightly derisively. It could have been envy. He'd had a dry spell of late. 'I don't know, but apparently she was a looker. Sounds like you blew it though, mate.'

I didn't know how to respond, so instead I said: 'You'll be in the Rose and Crown later?'

'Course. Arsenal – Man U.' He made it sound like I'd lost the plot.

'Right,' I said. 'I'll be there.'

I hung up and walked on down the hill into the Ville Basse, lost in thought. The quaint houses below were bizarrely juxtaposed with the giant, rusty-red bridge that led away from the far end of town. The big 'Red Bridge' connected the town with a set of mirrored office towers on the near horizon; through the snow, these monuments to finance (or the EU or whatever) appeared like some lost city in the sky.

The snow was falling thick and fast now. Descending the hill carefully, so as not to slip on the treacherously slick pavement, I dialled Claire's number.

The phone rang through to her voicemail, but I didn't want to leave a message. What more was there to say? She'd ended things, yet now wanted us to try again – or did she? I'd never known a woman to give so many mixed messages. She was the one who'd encouraged me to work at this company, to move on up the ladder, only to then claim that I'd wrecked everything by moving to Luxembourg.

I was still befuddled as I entered our modern office building, fishing around again for my security pass. It had slipped back into the jacket lining. I navigated my way through the little turnstile and onto the lower floor level, swiping in through two security doors. The rows of workstations lay eerily quiet and dark with the electric blinds closed.

At my desk, I logged on to my computer. I noted that there was a light on in the far corner office: Charlotte Newbury's. Charlotte ran the executive recruiting team and still did some recruiting herself ('for the senior leadership team' – she was always quick to distinguish her recruits from the merely functional managers that I worked on). Ours was a big company, with offices across Europe and lots of executives needed for the different locations.

Charlotte was my direct boss, and she could certainly be bossy. I considered leaving before she saw me. Not feeling at my most coordinated, I didn't want to deal with her, but I did need to update the system with a critical position we'd just opened up. If all went well I'd be out of there in ten minutes and she'd never know.

My machine was running as slow as me. It took several minutes for the primary-coloured Microsoft Office logo to appear. Probably software updates doing their updating.

I opened up my email. There was a typically curt message from the Vice President of Business Development, Mike Duchelle, asking me where we were with recruiting the Head of REE. (How the company loved its acronyms, like a new language to be learned, or one that keeps out the uninvited.) 'REE' is Russia and Eastern Europe. Business was booming out there, oil money and the like sloshing in.

There was also an email from Charlotte: had I followed up on the LinkedIn profile of the REE candidate that she'd sent me?

I clicked open the link in the email.

Up came the profile of one Yekaterina Novakovich. I leaned in to examine the woman's profile photo. She had big, bright eyes, giving me a slight underlook. God, no one on LinkedIn looked this good; her face was perfectly oval-shaped, her fair hair silky and straight.

She looked familiar. How old was she? Her profile didn't say, but from her Harvard graduation date I narrowed her age down to late twenties or early thirties. I tried to work out whether I'd seen her before, or whether some part of my primal brain was simply wired to look for a face like hers. She had a coy smile, full lips . . . and all the while she was looking up at me, knowingly.

The rest of her profile was bulletproof: after Harvard she'd been at McKinsey, and then risen swiftly through the ranks of EM Bank, one of Moscow's biggest. Her contacts for the role would be *im-pe-ccable*, as they say here in French.

I couldn't help looking again at her face, those eyes.

Let me tell you: headhunting is just like the dating game. Both rely on the art of seduction. And while I hadn't exactly excelled at either, I hadn't done so badly, in spite of the annoying attacks of scruples that I suffered at the least convenient of times.

I was beginning to compose an email to Yekaterina when I detected a familiar presence at my shoulder, along with a waft of expensive scent.

'Have you followed up on the LinkedIn profile of the REE candidate as I asked?' Charlotte said.

Never mind a 'hello'.

'Charlotte,' I said, clearing my throat. 'Didn't see you come in.' I turned and smiled.

Charlotte was as English as could be, bearing an uncanny physical resemblance to the American-born actress Gillian Anderson. The air held still around her, with her too-together look, frosty-eyed stare and puckered upper lip.

'Well?' she demanded.

I gestured at the screen. 'I'm following up with *le candidat* right now.'

'*La candidate*,' she corrected me.

She hovered and I deliberated whether to continue typing. I felt like I'd been caught in the middle of writing a personal email or something.

'I got a message about it from Mike,' I said. Mike was the head of Business Development. It was interesting watching Charlotte and him vie for seniority. 'Do you want me to update him?'

'No,' she said. 'I'll do that.'

'OK,' I said. 'Can I ask you a question?'

There was a glimmer in her eyes; I took that to mean yes.

'Why are we prioritising this position over all the other open ones?'

She continued looking at me, and finally said: 'It's a very competitive space.'

I waited for her to go on, but she didn't.

'OK.' My fingers hesitatingly found the keyboard once more.

Charlotte leaned in over my shoulder. 'Don't fuck it up, Mr Thorneycroft,' she breathed into my ear. Then she strode back to her office in her high boots, tight jeans and furry waistcoat; her expensive perfume lingered.

Blinking hard, I finished typing my overture to Yekaterina Novakovich.

The sky was half-light as I left the office, reminding me of my student days in Glasgow, where it was so far north that if you slept in too late, it was already dark again. I could hear the dark, icy waters sluicing down the Alzette; sometimes it felt like a flash flood could sweep it all away – all those corporate schemes and designs. Wouldn't be such a bad thing for me if it did.

On the sides of the valley were garden allotments and, higher up one side, what looked to be a woodsman's cottage, smoke drifting from the roof. Behind, in the distance, were the floodlit ramparts of the castle. It all looked like a scene from an old folk tale. I was deliberating whether to walk back up the hill right away, or stop for a late lunch at Mousel's, a traditional Luxemburgish *cantine* that served roast pig. I was famished. But I remembered that Mousel's was closed on Sundays, and I'd agreed to meet Phil at the Rose and Crown in time for kick-off. He would be deep into his first pint by now.

I trudged back up the hill, still thinking about the previous night's events, when my phone rang. The number was withheld. At first I let it ring, the falling snow turning to tiny water droplets on the keys of my BlackBerry. But something told me to take the call.

'Nick Thorneycroft,' I answered. I'd perfected this happy-chappy tone, which had worked well when I'd been a sportswriter.

I heard someone speaking away from the phone, then: 'Hello?'

A woman's voice.

'Who is this?' I asked.

'Kate Novakovich.'

The candidate. 'Hello,' I said, surprised. 'So glad you called. That was quick!'

'I read your email. I hope speaking on a Sunday is not inconvenient?' Her voice was low, and the way she rolled her *r*'s was distinctly Russian.

'No, it's great to hear from you –'

'I would like to apply for the position.'

'OK,' I said, bemused that she hadn't asked any questions first, but glad to be able to update Charlotte and Mike about her interest. 'Why don't you send over your CV?'

'I have already received other job offer. So it is best if I come for interview right away. Is it possible?'

'It's possible,' I said, gathering my thoughts, 'but I'll need to check schedules and come back to you.' I tried to make light of it. 'Can we know who we're up against?'

'Please say again?'

'Who else has made you an offer?'

'This I cannot say,' she said. 'But it is a very generous offer.'

They always were, I thought, while promising to get back to her as soon as possible.

Xanant

By the time I reached the Rose and Crown I'd confirmed that Charlotte and Mike were both available tomorrow to interview Yekaterina – or Kate, as she'd called herself. While there were others who'd be on the interview loop, these two executives would make the final decision.

I felt buoyant as I sat down beside Phil at a small table near the bar. Surprisingly, there were only a handful of people there that day: a trio of English lads I'd seen before, and an older couple who I didn't recognise, and who looked distinctly uncomfortable with the loud volume of the game, the roar of the crowd and the sharp excitement of the commentary. Dealing with work had made me late and the match was already underway at a sunny, if frigid-looking, Old Trafford.

Phil greeted me reproachfully. He had thin, severe lips and a pinched nose, with a permanently pensive look behind his frameless glasses. As I'd expected, he was well into his first pint.

'Sorry mate,' I said, pulling off my jacket. 'Get you another one?' I pointed to his glass and went to the bar, where I asked Linette, the barmaid, for another Bofferding for him and a pint of Okult Blanche for myself, plus two packets of plain crisps. It felt nice to come home . . . to a good Premier League game, the Arse taking on the big team, the score nil-nil fourteen minutes in, Fergie's team moving the ball around energetically, and Arsène Wenger appearing on the touchline in a long vinyl jacket that resembled a sleeping bag.

For me, football was an allegory for life. So much was decided by the managers before the game even began.

I took the pints over to our table and opened both packets of crisps, then took the head off the satisfyingly sudsy pint.

'I had to go into the office,' I said by way of explanation for my tardiness. 'Doesn't look like I missed a lot.'

On cue, Alex Ferguson appeared with a face the colour of beetroot, his rosacea inflamed by the cold and the lack of goals, no doubt; he was working his chewing gum hard.

'Cheers,' Phil said, accepting the drink.

'We've got a key candidate on the hook,' I explained further. 'G'on!' I suddenly heard myself yelling as Theo Walcott broke forward, snatching away a mistimed pass deep in Man U's half – only to scuff the ball wide of the post. The camera caught Wayne Rooney yelling at his teammates, looking more than ever like Shrek.

'Which position?' Phil asked.

For a second, I thought he was talking about the game.

I wasn't supposed to discuss the specifics of recruiting, but Phil and I were past that point. He'd been with the company for over four years and I'd found his perspective to be invaluable during the short time I'd known him.

'She's a candidate for the REE spot that just opened up. She looks like a good fit.'

'She's fit?' he misheard me.

Phil's luck with the ladies had been preserved only by his new black Maserati – a product of his stock-option payouts.

And those stock options were something I'd become all too familiar with, forming as they did a key part of the incentive offer that we put together for potential new recruits. What would Kate Novakovich get? A tidy sum, if I had anything to do with it. Why take the risk of losing her?

'You'll meet her soon enough,' I said. 'I hope,' I added, thinking about our phone conversation an hour earlier.

'Is there a visa problem or something?' Phil asked.

'She has another offer.'

'Happens, when they're good. From where?'

'She didn't say.'

'She wouldn't,' he remarked. 'Probably Xanant.'

I paused – my pint midway to my lips. 'Who?'

'Don't you know about Xanant?'

'No.'

'Payment processor in Russia, state-owned. Making major moves in the space.' He picked at the remaining crisps, transfixed by the screen. From nowhere, Paul Scholes had knocked a perfectly weighted pass into the penalty box, van Persie flicking it in.

The trio of lads at the nearby table erupted. Fergie was out of his seat with fists held high in jubilation. Fuck.

Something about Phil's remark hit home too. Suddenly, I could see Kate Novakovich working for some extension of the Russian state, a femme fatale honeypot, every Western man's fantasy of the elusive Russian beauty . . .

'Word is, they might be trying to buy us,' Phil went on.

'A Russian state company, buying *us*?'

'Yeah,' he said, scrunching up the empty crisp packet. 'They're big.'

'How do you know all this?' I asked him. He was merely a project or programme manager, after all.

He gave me a look, like: *How could you* not *know?*

I thought again about the events of the last twenty-four hours.

'Listen,' I said, eyeing Linette, the English lads and then the older couple, who'd stuck around. 'What happened last night? You said you left me in Zin Zen, but – '

'Mate, you left *me* in Zin Zen. You were that wasted you don't remember?'

I shook my head. 'I ended up at the casino. Only, no . . . I *don't* remember.'

'You must remember, if you know you ended up there.'

'That's the thing.' I laughed. 'I found a receipt for a bottle of champagne and two sandwiches. No idea who had the other sandwich. I thought it might have been you.'

A wry smile played on his lips. 'You really *were* wasted. Maybe you ate both.'

It was possible.

We fell silent. Man U had dropped back, thwarting Arsenal's attacking play. Wenger looked to be praying now; this would be his third defeat on the trot.

I felt in my pockets for the receipt, but it wasn't there. Must have left it in my bedroom.

'Maybe it was someone else's receipt,' I said. 'Maybe it

was sitting on the back seat of a taxi or something, and I picked it up by mistake.'

'Life's mysteries . . .' Phil said.

'Should be possible to find out,' I persevered. 'What venue has more security cameras than a casino?'

A little known fact I'd learned since working for this company: casinos had their own payment systems. Handling all that cash was too central, too strategic.

'I think we handle the payments for Ducal Casino, don't we?' I went on. 'Who's the account manager?'

Phil looked at me. 'Interesting method of approach. It's Mike Duchelle.'

'Mike Duchelle . . . has the Ducal account?'

'He was an account manager before he got promoted. Those relationships stick.'

The idea of going to Mike about getting a contact at Ducal Casino to see security footage of me there wasted . . . no.

'Here's what's really odd,' I said, leaning in. 'When I woke up – at my gaff, this morning – there was a pair of women's knickers on the floor. No clue whose.'

I immediately sensed I'd made a mistake bringing this up, like I was rubbing salt in the wound by mentioning my sex life, or what Phil perceived it as being. I wanted to go on and show him the mark on my skin, hidden by the polo neck, but thought better of it.

'Guess you solved the mystery of who was eating the other sandwich in the casino then,' he said sharply. 'Either that, or the knickers belong to your landlady.'

He laughed, and I laughed too, but with a queasy feeling at the thought of Mme Doriot naked.

At that very moment, the door of the pub swung open and there was M. Doriot. He was on his own, and for a second I thought he was still in his PJs. His striped trousers were made from a strikingly similar material. Mme Doriot's handiwork maybe, or perhaps they'd come as a set.

The Rose and Crown was just two streets away from our apartment building, but what was he doing in an English pub – and on a match day? 'Nick,' he said, coming over, 'here you are.'

His cap and the shoulders of his hunting jacket were wet from the snow.

'Can I have a word with you?' he said.

'Sure.' I got up and guided him towards the bar. 'Do you want a drink?'

He thought about it. 'No. Madame Doriot is expecting me back.'

I was ready for a second Okult, and let Linette know as much. 'So what's up?'

He dropped his voice below the level of the TV. 'The police came, asking about you.'

I felt a thud in my chest and a hot, prickly sensation on my scalp.

'They were asking about the person climbing along the roof.'

'Right.' That person would have been me, rescuing Mischa. It was a relief of sorts, but then I realised that someone must have been watching from the buildings opposite. 'Who was it that called the police?'

Just then, there was an explosion of noise from the TV. Phil clapped. The Arsenal players were celebrating, but no one in particular – Man U must have scored an own goal. Sure enough, Fergie was sat glowering, arms crossed and eyes bulging.

M. Doriot said: 'It is best that you stay here while Mme Doriot deals with them. She is good at this. The Luxembourg police can be . . . persistent.'

'I was planning to,' I said, half-looking at the screen for the action replay, while wondering what a witness might have observed last night.

'What about your neck?' M. Doriot asked.

'Huh? Oh it's fine,' I said. 'Listen – last night, when I came in . . . did you see who I was with?'

M. Doriot did a double take. 'You don't know?'

I raised my new pint, by way of explanation. 'I'd had a good night.'

He chuckled. 'I saw only her back.'

'Well? What was her back like then?'

He moved his hands down in an hourglass shape. 'Not bad. Not bad at all. *Une belle blonde . . .*'

I thought of Kate Novakovich, and the flash of recognition I'd felt upon first seeing her photo.

'She seemed foreign, maybe,' M. Doriot added.

'Russian?' Damn it.

'Yes, maybe.'

The Loop

Monday morning came quickly, as it always does, and I walked to work over the Adolphe Bridge in the fresh snow. Stooping figures hurried along, silhouetted against distant street lamps: it was atmospheric, beautiful even, but I was too distracted by my aching back and shoulders.

Arsenal had lost in the end; it's an act of masochism, I know, to support a club that loses as consistently as they do. Meanwhile, Mme Doriot had fended off the police, as predicted by M. Doriot, and I'd arranged via the corporate travel agency's website for Kate Novakovich to check in that morning, putting her up in a hotel facing the bridge, on Boulevard FD Roosevelt.

She'd made her own flight arrangements. Had she already been in town on the Saturday night?

I crossed Boulevard FDR. It ran along the far lip of the Pétrusse valley, which looked like a white void in the snow.

Zin Zen had been closed yesterday evening, denying me the chance of asking the barmaid there about my mystery companion. After a sleepless night, I now stood in front of Kate Novakovich's hotel.

With its pink, neon roof sign, softened by the falling snow, the Grand Hotel Cravat looked like something straight out of an old spy story. Perhaps it felt familiar to her from life in Moscow – or at least how I imagined her life in Moscow to be, on the payroll of this firm Xanant or whatever the hell she was up to.

I approached the hotel entrance cautiously and peered into the lobby, with its buttery colours and faded Seventies decor. There was an elderly couple talking to the receptionist, and I allowed myself a moment to imagine this pair's life of retirement . . .

But there was no sign of Kate.

The time was 8.15 a.m., according to my watch, and she wasn't due for her first interview until 11 a.m. I stayed there for a full minute, held by the thought of her appearing in the lobby.

The hotel, I now saw, had its own faded, jet-set glamour (as do so many pockets of Luxembourg): an ageing brass plaque beside the door identified this as the home of the 'Rolls Royce and Bentley Enthusiasts' Club of Benelux'. It's funny what the conscious mind distracts itself with when the subconscious is working on a problem. I felt like I was missing something. Why would this woman have drugged *me*, only to show up for a professional interview two days later?

It was baffling.

Pulling my thick scarf tighter around my neck and the faded mark there, I walked on to the office, thinking about the day ahead. After Kate's interview with Mike Duchelle at 11 a.m., I would take her for an early lunch. Charlotte Newbury would resume the interrogation at 1 p.m. More interviews, then the debrief meeting, in which we would make our decision . . . I rubbed my face with my hands, feeling the raw coldness of the skin there, the weight of the tasks ahead of me, and descended the hill in the snow.

Darrel Casablancas, the recruitment coordinator, greeted me in the office lobby. He looked as camp as could be in his lime-green sweater and canary-yellow trousers.

'I got your emails,' he said tartly. 'From over the weekend, while I was away.' He folded his arms. 'How am I supposed to coordinate this way?'

'We have a couple of hours before she arrives,' I said. 'Walk with me.'

We swiped through the two security doors and went to my desk, Darrel noisily pulling up a chair. I took off my wet coat and scarf. There was that reluctant Monday morning hum about the place. The lights of Charlotte's office burned bright, and had probably been doing so since dawn. Should I go and talk to her, explaining the weekend's events? No, I'd sound crazy. So I reached for my notebook and divided one of the blank pages into quadrants.

'All the interviews are scheduled. I took care of that myself,' I said. I scribbled down the names and times in the top-left box.

'I see that,' Darrel said.

'The debrief I've set up, too, for six this evening,' I went on. That was the second quadrant.

'Right!'

'We need to start putting together an offer package,' I continued, with half an eye on Charlotte, who was pacing around her office with her headset on – some very important call, I imagined.

'Salary, bonus, stock options, relocation,' I continued. 'Make it the best we can for a Vice President position.'

'But we haven't decided to hire her yet.'

'We need to be ready.'

That left one quadrant empty.

Background checks.

Was there even time?

It's surprising, the length companies go to, researching executive recruits. It's not simply a case of checking for criminal convictions, poor credit scores or social media mishaps.

On one occasion, just after I'd joined the company, we'd engaged a former Belgian police captain – turned private investigator – to research a candidate we were considering for the position of Head of Benelux. It had been Charlotte's idea – based on what, I don't know. The candidate was brilliant on paper, a CEO of a small Brussels-based bank, and came with all the right recommendations. But the PI had found him visiting strip clubs and brothels on the outskirts of Antwerp. He'd followed him into one and discreetly taken photos of him getting down to it with a couple of prostitutes in a public, if dark, part of the club . . . one of whom looked suspiciously androgynous – male, the PI reckoned.

Look, whatever these executives got up to in their own time was their business. They had precious little time to start with. Our company could live with risk-taking behaviour in private; it was a common enough trait, even (or especially) among the more staid executives, as Phil once told me. No, the real headache was the scope for blackmail. If those photos ever made their way into the wrong hands, what could a blackmailer extract from the Head of Benelux? The answer was a decent amount, via the bank data that flowed through our systems, which this guy would have had access to. The tax position of large corporations, the wealth of certain high-net-worth individuals, even their spending habits – there were plenty of options for exploiting the data.

'Well?' Darrel was saying.

I looked again at her CV.

St Petersburg University, Harvard, McKinsey, EM Bank. It was bulletproof. Or was it? Before Harvard there had been a ten-month gap. Maybe just time off? She didn't strike me as the sort of person to cut loose. I was thinking about what this unexplained gap might mean, when I noticed from the corner of my eye that Charlotte was off the phone.

'Hold on,' I told Darrel.

I went over to her office and tapped on the window. She barely registered me, but I took that as enough of an invitation to enter.

She was dressed in a turquoise silk blouse, which had what looked like shoulder pads. A photo on her glass desk faced away from me; I'd never seen who (or what) was in it. She locked her office at night, of course.

'Looks like we're all set with Kate,' I said.

'Kate?' she cocked her head a fraction.

'Yekaterina,' I corrected myself.

'Do you two know each other?'

'No,' I said.

Her frosty eyes flicked down to my neck, then back up to

hold my face. The mark had pretty much gone, thank God, but it was still just visible, like a fading love bite.

'Look,' I pulled out her CV from under my arm. 'There's a gap here, before she went to Harvard. Do we need to look into that?'

'You tell me,' she said.

'I . . . There's more,' I said. 'There's Xanant to consider.'

I don't know why I even said that. I only know that I'd needed to say something. Now her eyes were boring into mine.

'How come you know about Xanant?'

For a second I couldn't remember anything about Xanant. Lack of sleep, maybe. No wait – Phil had mentioned something about it in the Rose and Crown.

'How could I *not* know about Xanant?' I bluffed. 'We just need to know that there's not an issue there. Unknown unknowns and all that.'

I had no idea what I was talking about now, but Charlotte was nodding slowly.

She crossed her arms.

'What did you have in mind?' she asked.

'I – I was thinking about the guy we used for the Benelux candidate that time and wondering whether there's not someone here in Luxembourg we could deploy. Just to make sure. That everything's fine.'

'Okay,' she said. 'Let me think about that.'

'Sure,' I said, checking my watch. 'She'll be here soon.'

Ordinarily, it would have been the recruitment coordinator who went to collect the candidate and shepherded her around the interviews, but I'd relieved Darrel of that responsibility. Darrel was fuming by now, of course – probably writing hate posts about me on the Internet, but I couldn't let him get in the way. There was a real-life mystery that needed solving.

I walked to the lobby and found a tall woman facing away from me beside the reception desk. She had her weight ever-so-slightly on one shoe – a high heel. Her hip was cocked, accentuating her curves; she wore a black, figure-hugging jacket and skirt; her straight, silky blonde hair fell evenly over both shoulders. Jesus. Was this the view that M. Doriot had seen on the stairs of our building on Saturday night?

Liesl, the receptionist, smiled warmly as I approached.

'Hello,' I said, unconsciously deepening my voice.

The tall woman turned.

It was one of those moments in life I'll never forget. Her face was the same one I'd seen on LinkedIn, only it looked brighter as her big amber eyes flashed: she was absolutely stunning. I felt a wrench at the base of my stomach – a yearning, I suppose, for something I instinctively knew I'd never possess.

'Hi,' she said, smiling widely. 'Kate Novakovich.'

I felt my heart beating fast and was in no doubt that, had I seen this woman out in a bar and thought I was in with even half a chance, I'd have gone for it.

'Nick Thorneycroft,' I said. 'Good to meet you.' I shook her hand. 'How was your trip?'

She returned my handshake firmly, saying: 'It is nice to be here.'

I paused, trying to slow things down, stay on top of the situation. Did she just avoid the travel question? 'And the hotel is all right?' I went on.

'It is good,' she said. 'It has a balcony, a view.'

My heart was still beating too quickly. 'Have they given you a temporary security pass?' I looked at Liesl, who nodded. I'd drawn myself up taller, I realised, with my shoulders back; Kate was only a couple of inches shorter than me in her heels.

Another agonising pause.

'Well, why don't you follow me?' I said, finally.

She reached for a black roller bag, the fabric of her skirt tightening around her hips and thighs. I thought of offering to help, but decided against it. She straightened, and smiled again.

We walked to the interview room, me swiping through the doors and holding them open for her. I'd fallen under a spell, bewitched into silence and unable to shake the suspicion that this woman had cornered me in a bar and drugged me, then returned to my apartment and searched it. I needed to get a private investigator on to her – under the cover of Charlotte Newbury's approval and paranoia. This was a game of chess, and it was my move.

'Here we go,' I said. It was a room in the south-west corner of the building, overlooking the river. Just outside the window, fat snowflakes twirled. The overhead lights came on from a motion sensor, startling me and dimming the view outside. Kate was setting her bag down in one corner.

The bright room had an elongated, blond-wood table

with chairs around it and a grey Polycom conference phone. There wasn't much else, except her. I could smell her scented perfume, or shampoo. Cinnamon. She was still turned away from me, reaching for a writing pad from the front pocket of her roller bag.

'Would you like a drink?' I asked.

Had I already asked her that question, late on Saturday night?

'Some water please,' she replied, not meeting my gaze.

As I went to get it, I remembered that I wasn't meant to leave a candidate alone, but reasoned that the little kitchen was only down the corridor.

Coming the other way was the imposing form of Mike Duchelle.

'Hey!' he called out, ten yards away.

I know I've mentioned Mike already, but I should say a bit more about him. He was a Biz Dev guy of the old school, probably in his late forties, maybe early fifties. American-Italian in appearance. He had a full head of black hair (surely dyed), a craggy face, and a larger-than-life presence, always.

He'd treated me as one of the guys ever since I'd explained the rules of rugby to him in a crowded bar in town one night, drawing parallels with American football. At one point, from nowhere, he'd produced an *actual* American football and thrown it very fast and accurately at the glass-laden bar top where I was waiting to buy a round of drinks.

Miraculously, I'd managed to catch it.

Mike slapped me on the shoulder. 'This the room you got for Katrina an' I?'

'Indeed,' I said. 'You have a copy of her résumé?'

He tapped his temple with a fat forefinger. 'It's all up here.' Then he winked, and I felt myself wince from some sort of unexpected possessiveness – competition from the larger male maybe – or, more likely, the sense of foreboding that was creeping through my veins. Mike closed the door behind him and, this time, I didn't fetch Kate a drink.

Just Lunch

When I got back to my desk, I found that Claire had called me three times. I opened Outlook and immediately saw her email with the subject line: *We need to talk*.

> *Nick,*
> *I've tried calling you.*
> *I have news, which you should know.*
> *It would be good if we could arrange to talk sooner rather than later. I'll leave it up to you to decide when, exactly.*
> *x C*

I sighed and felt my shoulders sag. What news? How so very Claire, I thought, to give me the illusion of choice. 'Up to you to decide . . .' Sure. Like the way she'd encouraged me out there to Lux, only to attack me for then doing so.

What made this woman tick?

I thought about her parents, and her dad in particular, who she hadn't spoken with in years. One time, early on in our relationship, I'd asked about him and . . . well, talk about being given short shrift. Clearly, something had gone very wrong there in the past.

My mind was whirring. There was too much going on. *What news?* I found myself repeating, nearly hitting delete and then deciding not to. It felt like an act of provocation. Which was ridiculous; she'd never know . . . though Claire did have this ability to feel omnipresent in my life. I yearned for the straightforwardness of Kate, her Russian directness. Or rather, how I imagined Kate *could* be, when not drugging men and leaving underwear in their apartments.

The best course of action was to go outside for a cigarette. I rarely smoked, especially in the depths of winter, and I didn't have a pack on me. But I knew that there would be the familiar knot of people huddled near reception, and I could cadge a smoke off one of them.

Sure enough, as I walked through reception, pulling up my collar, I spied Bjorn Hardwick on the gloomy other side of the window. Bjorn ran 'Product Platform Payment Program Projects', whatever that was, and I'd only just emailed him about interviewing Kate at 2 p.m., after Charlotte's slot.

'Hey Nick,' he said as I went outside, his breath condensing. Thick flakes of snow were settling in his fair hair and eyelashes.

'Hey Bjorn. Got a spare cigarette? I left mine at home.'

'Sure.' He offered me his pack.

Forget the airless world of LinkedIn; the smoker's colony was where the real networking got done among people from across the company. Not to mention the employees from the building just across the plaza – whenever they finally arrived. Speculation was rife as to who the new tenants of Building Two would be.

'Would be nice if it was Hawaiian Tropic,' Bjorn was

saying in his flat Scandinavian accent. 'The modelling department, that is.'

He wasn't known for his subtlety, Bjorn.

'Talking of which, I hear your interview candidate is hot,' he said to me. 'I can't do that interview time, but I could meet with her for dinner?'

He spoke in such a deadpan voice that I never knew whether he was joking or not.

'The debrief is at 6 p.m.,' I said, taking a deep drag on my cigarette. 'It might be a bit late.'

'You're not messing around with this one, are you?' Bjorn said, eyes narrowing, surveying the corporate, snowy wilderness of the plaza and the unoccupied building opposite.

'Could you do a half-hour interview? Whatever suits you, Bjorn,' I patted him on the shoulder, stamping out my cigarette in the snow. The nicotine was starting to turn my stomach.

I walked inside, putting a piece of gum into my mouth, and made my way back to the interview room. I knocked on the door and opened it a couple of inches. Laughter, from both Mike and Kate. Her eyes flashed at me.

'Hey sport!' Mike turned around. 'That time already?' He stood, and clasped her hand in his. 'Well, it was great to meet you. I hope to see you around soon . . .'

He ushered me outside, out of earshot.

'Close her,' he instructed.

'The rest of her interviews are this afternoon; the debrief's at 6 p.m. –'

'Who else is interviewing her?'

'Charlotte, Bjorn Hardwick –'

He waved his hand dismissively. 'Move the debrief up. No later than mid-afternoon. We need to get her on board. Now.'

'OK,' I said. No candidate had ever been fast-tracked quite like this before, to my knowledge. 'Will you enter your interview notes in the system?'

He tapped his temple with his forefinger. 'I'll bring them to the debrief with me.' With that he slapped me on the shoulder and strolled off down the corridor.

I'd booked lunch at a restaurant just the other side of the Alzette River, a place called the Mansfeld.

As we walked over the little bridge, I asked her how it had gone with Mike.

She was silent for a good few seconds, then said: 'I do not know how one building can contain so much personality!' She laughed in a curiously childlike way, almost with a sense of wonder.

And I couldn't help laugh too.

We walked through the stone arch at the front of the restaurant, to the courtyard area with its wintery plane trees – snow piled up on their branches – and then into the warmth of the building itself. It was the remnant of some vast residence owned by a sixteenth-century governor of Luxembourg; he'd fled the country with two hundred creditors besieging the place, or so I'd been told by a pleasant young waitress the first time I'd visited. The lower bar area featured vivid neon blue – the kind of experimental updating you tended to find around Luxembourg – but the dining area upstairs showed off the thick stone walls that bore witness to the building's true past.

The same pleasant waitress seated us and gave us menus. I was focused entirely on Kate, who was looking out the window at the Alzette, her amber eyes glowing.

'Would you like to start with an aperitif?' the waitress asked.

'Sparkling water,' Kate answered.

I'd half a mind to order a beer – a Chimay or something similarly strong, but I restrained myself. 'Make that a bottle.'

Is this how I'd ordered the Lanson at Ducal Casino, thirty-six hours before?

'Have we met before?' I suddenly asked.

Her gaze was still on the river outside.

'I don't think so,' she said evenly, without a trace of hesitation. There was merely the faintest, confused crinkling of her brow.

If she was lying, she was damn good at it.

I took the napkin from the table and placed it on my lap, then broke open a small roll of bread that the waitress had offered. If I was to close her, as Mike had instructed, then I needed to understand her remuneration expectations, so that we knew where to pitch our offer.

There was a stocky man sitting at the table behind Kate, pin-neat in his dark suit. It was hard to find a place in the area to eat where you didn't risk being overheard, but he looked to be consumed by his veal: the typical, Luxemburgish businessman.

'But this place feels familiar. It reminds me of home,' she said.

I turned to see the view of the Alzette she was gazing at, then looked back to her: 'Moscow?'

'No, east of there. Kuznetsk.' She corrected herself: 'Novokuznetsk.'

I tried to visualise the vastness of Russia – its eastward sprawl around the globe, all the way to the tip of America – and where, in that land mass, she might have grown up.

'What is your home town like?'

'It is on the Tom River. It is a steel town, now.'

A connection, then. Luxembourg, too, had once had a sizeable steel industry.

She paused and explained: 'At first, it was a Cossack fortress, Kuznetsk. It is an area rich in minerals, so it was turned into an industrial centre, Stalinsk.' She paused again. 'My grandfather helped the town to reclaim its old name. Novokuznetsk – *New* Kuznetsk.'

The water arrived, fizzing. I couldn't take my eyes off her.

'What did your grandfather do?'

'He worked in the steel industry. He and my father.'

I slowed down my chewing of the bread. Did she know that I, too, came from a line of steelworkers?

'My father and grandfather worked in steel. In England.'

'Oh,' she said, taking a neat sip of water, her lips moistened. 'Where?'

'Place called Blackburn. You wouldn't have heard of it.'

But I bet she had heard of it. I bet she knew all about my father having worked for Walkersteel, before it was bought out by British Steel back in the late Eighties, and how he got made redundant; I bet she knew that he was a big-boned, frightening man who didn't take well to unemployment; that Blackburn Rovers – whose team and stadium were rebuilt by the Walker brothers' cash windfall – were my inspiration to become a sportswriter, before I changed careers with Claire's encouragement. What *didn't* she know?

I looked down at the menu. The young waitress was back.

'What would you like?' I asked Kate.

She looked down, too. I told the waitress: 'For me, the *lieu noir en pannequet*. It's a fish, right? In pastry?'

The waitress nodded, and informed me that I'd had it there last time. I remembered it now, a rich man's fish and chips.

'*L'onglet de veau*,' Kate said. '*Mariné au paprika, avec pomme pont-neuf.*'

I saw from my Rolex that we'd been there twenty minutes already. I needed to get her back for Charlotte's interview, move the debrief forward . . .

She stretched out her hand, touching her fingertips to mine.

'You have steelmakers' hands,' she said.

Her fingers were so much more slender than my compact digits; so much smoother, compared to the thick veins on the back of my hand, the little dark hairs on my fingers. Her bare ring finger beckoned to me.

I couldn't play these games with her.

'I wanted to talk briefly about remuneration.' I changed the subject, withdrawing my hand. 'As you know, we're a fast-growing company. And we believe in the concept of ownership: that when you work here, you shouldn't feel like a tenant. So we emphasise stock options over base salary. It's important to consider the package in total. Of course, in your case, we would also offer a generous relocation package . . .'

She was looking out at the river again.

'I need to know what your remuneration expectations are, though,' I persisted. 'To make sure we're aligned.'

'You're asking me how much I expect to earn?' she asked, amused.

'Yes. That would be helpful.'

'What's my number?' she said and a smile broke over her lips.

'Yes,' I coughed slightly. The bread was making my throat dry. 'I need something to take back with me.'

She reached into her bag, producing a raspberry-coloured steel pen. Then, on the corner of the napkin, she wrote a number, beginning with 007. She laughed once more, showing a full set of white teeth; it was the prefix for dialling Russia.

She'd only given me her damn phone number.

And not the one on her CV.

I took her back across the river to the office, where Charlotte received her frostily.

Then I went straight to my computer and googled her again, this time adding the place name 'Novokuznetsk'. There was a Leonid Novakovich, who, I discovered in translation, had been in the Steel Secretariat of the local Communist party there – back in the Seventies and early Eighties.

Her grandfather?

I kept scrolling through the translated search results until a reference to the International Gymnastics Federation caught my eye. I clicked on it and a photo of a young girl with Kate's precise features appeared. She stood, slim-figured, beside a set of asymmetric bars.

Her eyes were calm yet determined. The tendons of her wrists showed prominently; her hands were chalky-white. She was smiling proudly as a stern man looked on. Her father? A trainer? I checked her CV; there was no mention of gymnastics in the interests or background sections. Perhaps she hadn't done any since the time this photo was taken.

Still, the article mentioned that she'd reached the highest level of the sport, locally at least.

I sat back, aware of the hypnotic clacking of my colleagues' keyboards, the urgency of the work getting done around me, the need to close my candidate.

Sitting forward again, I googled Novokuznetsk. From the map I could see that it was twice as far east of Moscow as Moscow was from Luxembourg – equidistant between Moscow and Alaska. Just north of Mongolia.

Absolute bloody middle of nowhere.

The civic flag showed a white horse leaping over a little building housing a steel furnace; was this a metaphor for Kate's life? Was she leaping from her provincial past to a bigger, better future? I couldn't help seeing associations with my own life, and me ending up in Luxembourg.

Then I noticed something else: Igor Strokan hailed from Novokuznetsk. We all know what has become of Strokan, the steel oligarch turned occupant of the Kremlin. I shouldn't have been so surprised that he'd risen from this kind of background. Jack and Fred Walker, Blackburn's steel magnates, had consorted with the biggest beasts of New Labour. One-time Home Secretary Jack Straw was still Blackburn's Member of Parliament.

But there was something else significant about Strokan's name coming up: the timing. He was up for re-election as President of Russia.

'*Le candidat*,' I couldn't help muttering under my breath. This time with the correct, masculine, form.

Debriefed

When her interview with Charlotte was over, I walked Kate over to Darrel Casablancas, who was to look after her.

'Perhaps you could take her for coffee?' I suggested.

He scowled and led her away.

Quickly, I printed off copies of Kate's CV and the outline remuneration proposal I'd put together. Then I hurried back to the meeting room – the same one we'd been using for the interviews.

As soon as I got there, I could tell that something was wrong. Mike Duchelle had arrived and was sat across from Charlotte, his large legs crossed, picking lint off his trousers. Charlotte was staring out into the gloom of the floor-to-ceiling windows. The floodlit castle appeared as a spectral blur, obscured by snow haze.

I could see from the little red light on the phone that they'd started a conference call, most likely with Global Compensation at our Maryland headquarters, for fast-track approval of the offer package.

'OK,' I said. It was my responsibility to lead the debrief. 'Thanks, everyone, for being available at such short notice. Perhaps we could start with everyone present saying whether they are inclined or not inclined to hire, and why.'

Charlotte ignored me, saying to Mike: 'We just can't take the risk. Not now. Not at this stage.'

There was a crackle on the conference line as someone began to speak, which Mike pre-empted: 'It's because we're at this stage that we *need* to take the risk.'

'We need to background her,' Charlotte was insisting. 'We need to run the usual checks.'

While I wasn't being allowed to lead the meeting, Charlotte seemed to be pushing my idea of getting an investigator involved, which could only bring answers.

'How long would it take?' Mike was asking.

'Depending on the location, a week or two at most. *At most*,' she repeated.

'That's too long.' Mike stood up, his bulk appearing in duplicate, reflected in the darkening glass of the window. He faced out towards the castle.

'What do we have so far?' a confident voice said on the phone.

It didn't sound like Global Comp. Maybe it was someone from Central Security. I no longer felt a part of this.

'Nothing,' Charlotte said. 'No references, no history – nothing.'

The rustling of pages came through over the phone. 'Unless her résumé's inaccurate, we can at least get her verified by Harvard admissions. Or the McKinsey alumni. There are enough of them around this place.'

Who was the Voice? His deep, leisured tones communicated seniority. I wanted to ask Mike or Charlotte, but it didn't feel like the right time to speak up. Sometimes it was better to be forgotten about.

'That would be a start,' Charlotte responded to the Voice.

'We should run whatever checks on her we can,' the Voice went on. 'But fast.' Then he changed tack. 'Do you have a sense for what business she could bring in? Mike, do you think she could get us EM Bank?'

'I do,' he said.

Charlotte spoke next. 'There's no question that she's strong, and a desirable asset right now. There's no question she could help us. The question is: could she also harm us?'

'If she's working for our competitor-friends in Luxembourg already?' the Voice clarified.

'Exactly,' Charlotte said.

'If she is, then that just shows the seriousness of their interest in the location.'

'If she already is, then how do we demonstrate the greater value of our business to them?'

'Others are interested in us too,' Mike intervened. 'It shows the others the value. They then show our competitor-friends . . .'

It was hard to keep up with the logic, the argumentation. But what was clear to me was that there was a much bigger game in play. From the Rose and Crown, Phil's words came back to me: 'Word is that Xanant might be trying to buy us.'

'The candidate wants to get here fast,' Mike was saying.

'Too fast,' Charlotte countered.

'She's being forced to choose,' Mike said. 'Hell, they're about to open up shop opposite!'

There was a reflective pause, in which I realised that he was talking about Building Two. This Russian state giant was about to set up on our doorstep. Smoke break was about to catch fire.

'Why don't we turn it around?' Mike said, ever the dealmaker. 'Say that we'll take her now, but pending full review of her credentials, and we reserve the right to end her employment without further compensation if there's a problem.'

'Trust, but verify,' the Voice said. 'I like that.'

'Do you have a problem with that approach?' Mike rounded on Charlotte.

'Keep it civil,' the Voice stepped in. 'We're still a team, and an independent one at that.'

'For now,' Mike added.

Charlotte said nothing, her upper lip more puckered than ever.

'But how much value could she bring us out in the marketplace?' The Voice returned to his previous subject. 'I'm still not clear from your interview, Mike. I don't seem to have your notes.'

'Yeah, sorry, I'll get those written up. But let me be clear: if we can tell a good story about how we're building a Russian and Eastern European practice, anchored by her? Shit . . . DAT, Ektrix, T Street – they'll all come running. They all want to be in on the action, the region. It'd only take one of them to get an auction going over us –'

'And the new neighbours must know that,' Charlotte said, nodding towards Building Two.

'Which is why they're after her,' the Voice said.

'Which is why she's eager to seal the deal with us,' said Mike.

'She'll be working for them soon enough anyway,' the Voice concluded, lightening the mood.

'When we're on the beach,' added Mike, grinning.

Whatever the endgame was between Mike, Charlotte and the Voice, it had precious little to do with me. They all had buckets of stock options – ownership stakes in the company – which would pay out handsomely if the company was acquired. Whereas I'd only recently joined, on a probationary basis, and had practically nothing to show for it. A pittance of stock grants.

As we walked out of the room, Mike came up alongside me.

'Hey, good work,' he said, putting his arm around my shoulder in a father-son sort of way. 'Well done for moving the ball forward on this one. Won't be forgotten.'

I didn't know what he meant by that – a bonus maybe? I thought to ask him for something else instead: the Ducal Casino contact so that I could check the CCTV cameras from Saturday night. Only, I knew how opposed he was to checking up on Kate now: he just wanted things to be done and dusted.

'Anytime,' I said.

Darrel Casablancas was standing in front of us, his trimmed eyebrows raised inquiringly.

'We're in good shape,' I said. 'Where's Kate?'

'She was done for the day, so she left,' Darrel replied. 'She wanted to see the town.'

'You just let her go?' I said.

'Her interviews were over!'

'OK, OK. Could you just reach out to a couple of the McKinsey alums, check Kate's history? Also Harvard – the admissions office.'

I was done for the day, too. Global Comp, back in Maryland, would take over on the offer package, pushing it through approvals.

Darrel, Mike and I went our separate ways. I noticed that Charlotte had stayed in the meeting room. Maybe she'd hung on to the room for her next conference call. Or maybe she was just thinking.

I went back to my desk and printed off Kate's LinkedIn profile – the photo specifically – and then I snuck out, coat and scarf under my arm. I put them on in reception and hurried out into the darkness. Building Two loomed emptily, expectantly. It would be quite the little campus that the combined company would inherit down here.

Walking up the hill, I tried Phil on his mobile. He didn't pick up, so I left him a message asking whether he was available for a quick drink after work. I had questions for him about the way all this was going down.

Then I reached into my coat pocket and pulled out the napkin that Kate had written her phone number on. She was the person I really wanted to have a drink with.

Her number was blotted. I dialled it and she picked up.

'Hello?'

'It's Nick. Nick Thorneycroft. How are you?'

'Fine,' she said.

I could hear street sounds. She was outside somewhere.

'You left the office this afternoon before I had chance to

say goodbye. I just wanted to check that all went well this afternoon.'

'Yes,' she replied. 'Very well. And you?'

'Yeah, great . . . You had a good day?'

'I enjoyed it, yes. It felt good.'

There was a pause, pregnant with possibility.

'We're just reviewing everything. Listen –' I wanted so badly to ask her out for a drink, but it was too risky. The stakes were too high at the office. So I said: 'Why don't you come back to the office tomorrow morning? When do you have to leave again?'

'I have not yet decided. But I will see you tomorrow?'

'Yes,' I said. 'Come in at ten a.m. Have a lie-in.'

'I'm sorry?'

There was a beeping horn in the background on her end. A truck reversing, maybe.

'Never mind. See you at ten.'

'OK,' she said. 'I will see you then.'

I ended the call, stopping for a moment under a street lamp. The old town winked back below.

I began walking, faster; it was another few minutes before I crested the hill and found myself in front of the pink sign of the Hotel Cravat.

I entered the warmth of the lobby, aware that I might run into Kate. A few minutes before, she'd been out on one of the town's streets; there were only so many streets in Luxembourg, so she couldn't have been that far away. If I saw her, what would I say?

The receptionist, a swarthy-skinned man with dark eyes, looked up at me. I cleared my throat. 'I'm interested in staying here, but wondered whether you had any rooms with a balcony and a view?'

That was how Kate had described her room.

I looked over my shoulder, towards the dark Pétrusse Valley and the Adolphe Bridge. She hadn't appeared.

'Many of the rooms have views,' the receptionist said, looking at me puzzled, as if to say: *Why would anyone want a balcony in winter*?

'This town is so beautifully lit at night,' I explained.

He looked down at a screen, or a reservations book maybe – it was hidden from view by the top of the reception desk.

'We have only one room with a balcony. Room 550.'

Bingo.

'Could I see it? If I like it, I'd want to book it.'

He shook his head. 'It is occupied.'

I looked over my shoulder. The elderly couple I'd seen in the lobby that morning had entered, laden with shopping bags and Christmas gifts. There was no concierge, and I felt the urge to help them.

'Till when?' I asked.

'Next week. The fifteenth. Would you like to reserve it from that date?'

Kate had only been booked in for two nights; had she rebooked it herself?

'No,' I said, 'I'll need something before then, but many thanks for checking.'

I walked back towards the front door, but turned sharply to my left, as if distracted by the table of paper brochures and tourist cards on that side of the lobby. From there, I made my way around to the single elevator door, out of sight of the receptionist.

The old-fashioned lift took an age to arrive. I still couldn't think what I'd do if Kate suddenly came up behind me.

I clattered the old door open and shut it behind me, hitting the '5' button. The lift jolted into motion, ascending slowly. After a minute or two of whining cables, I opened the door onto the fifth floor. But I could only see two rooms, and neither one was 550.

How could it not exist?

I took the stairs down to the fourth floor and found a corridor through to the other side of the building, then stairs back up to five, with a separate lift that I'd somehow missed in reception. I must have taken the service lift. A sign guided me along another corridor to room 550.

I didn't know what I expected to happen at this point. Maybe I hoped to find a maid doing a late room clean – that there'd be some way to wangle my way in, just as Kate had done in my apartment two days before. I tried the door handle: of course, it was locked.

Perhaps I hoped to be caught by her.

I heard the lift door clatter open and the sound of footsteps – multiple footsteps – along with two voices, one being hers.

I felt my heart thump. They were out of my view, but wouldn't be for long. There was just the continuation of the L-shaped corridor, at the join of which was room 550 – and myself. The corridor terminated at another room, 553. I walked towards the dead end, my neck prickling.

When I got there, I patted my pockets down as if searching for a key. I felt my palms sweating, my senses supernaturally alive.

'*Da, da,*' I heard behind me. I could tell from the man's footfall that he was heavyset.

'*Nick!*' – I kept expecting to hear, but instead there was only the man speaking Russian. Her boyfriend come to join her? To scope out Luxembourg?

It was a flinty, ill-tempered conversation. Mercifully, they sounded too preoccupied to notice me, or rather the back of me, ten yards away. Who was he? I heard their key turn in the lock, then the door opening and banging shut behind them, finally.

I heaved a big sigh, still feeling my heart beating hard.

The door handle of 553 suddenly moved, as if on its own, and there in front of me was the startled, birdlike face of the woman I'd seen in the lobby, one half of the elderly couple.

'Wrong room,' I said, turning on my heel.

I bowed my head as I walked back past 550; I could hear the muffled voices of Kate and her mystery man. I wanted to stop and listen, but I knew the old dear I'd surprised would still be watching me.

Twice I'd been lucky, in as many minutes; I couldn't rely on a third instance.

The Offer

I walked straight out of the hotel lobby and into the evening darkness, going just a few doors up the street to Zin Zen.

The swanky, black-and-mirrored interior was subdued at this hour; it was a Saturday night hotspot, not a Monday night after-work hangout, but it was at least open now. There were two staff members at the bar: a chiselled-jawed guy reading a magazine studiously, as if his life depended on it, and a platinum blonde rearranging bottles of champagne in a claw-foot bath parked beside the bar, the ice slushing, bottles clanking.

Nothing was coming back to me from Saturday night. There was an old Massive Attack track on the sound system, 'Unfinished Sympathy', turned down low. Everything in this town felt decades out of date, but it reminded me, melancholically, of my student days. I felt a stab of panic at my amnesia being so total.

I reached into my inside pocket and pulled out Kate's LinkedIn profile picture, which I'd printed off.

'Hi,' I said to the blonde bartender. She had almond-shaped eyes – amber-coloured like Kate's, only colder.

'I wonder if you could answer a question. I'm trying to trace a missing person. If I show you a photo, could you tell me if you recognise her from Saturday night?'

She looked appraisingly at the photo, like she was sizing up a competitor, then at me again, like I was another challenge to be handled.

'No,' she said simply.

'No . . . you don't recognise her?'

'No, I can't tell you. I wasn't working that night. There are different staff on weekends, you will need to ask them.'

'When will they be working again?'

'Thursday. And Friday and Saturday.'

I thought about ordering a drink, a glass of champagne even, to break the ice – also to see if it prompted any memories. But I knew this endeavour was doomed. I could ask her to give the photo of Kate to the other bartenders, along with my phone number, but something told me not to do that – not to be seen to be asking around. I needed to bide my time, to come back later in the week. With Phil, who'd spoken to one of the bar staff in question. One of them had told him I'd left with 'a looker' – or maybe Phil had paraphrased it. I scanned the quiet bar once more for any clues, then nodded my thanks and left.

Phil had agreed to meet me at six in the Rose and Crown, and so I started to make my way there. I walked across the bridge; the snow had turned into a misty, freezing rain and the pavement was slushy. Halfway across, I turned and looked at the pink glow of Kate's hotel, counterpointed by the orange blur of the big cathedral. I wiped my eyes to see, letting my imagination picture her making up, making out even, with the mystery man in her room.

I entered the Rose and Crown with relief – at its warmth and the friendly smile of Linette, owl-like behind the bar, her hair fluffed up.

'An Okult Blanche?' she asked.

'How did you guess?' I sat down heavily on a bar stool, the red light of my BlackBerry blinking furiously. 'And one for yourself.'

'Ta, love.'

As she poured my pint, I checked my email. Global Comp had already put together the offer for Kate and it was going through the rounds of approval fast. It was a very generous offer: several times my own package, but you could never afford to think like that as a headhunter. You just had to keep your targets in the cross hairs.

Linette presented me with a pint. 'Here you go.'

'Cheers.' I raised it and gulped down a couple of mouthfuls, sighing. Suddenly I caught Linette looking at me, like my mam might have done years before.

'You're looking tired, Nick.'

'Didn't get much sleep last night.' I gave her a broad smile.

'You should find a nice lady and settle down. A man your age . . .' She tutted, shaking her head.

I agreed and felt another stab at the thought of Kate, how our fingers had touched at lunchtime. I wondered about Claire, too, and her news.

I was craving something sweet, a crêpe perhaps. That, or a cigarette.

The door swung open and in came Phil, peering confusedly through his misted glasses. I raised a hand.

He wiped his glasses, put them back on and looked at me.

'Second time in two days,' he said, mounting the bar stool beside me. 'Aren't I a lucky chap? What's up?'

I got him a drink.

We had the preliminary chit-chat – football and all that. Then: 'I had the strangest interview debrief this afternoon.'

'For the REE role?' he said.

'Yeah.'

I looked around, but the place was practically empty; just a bulky older chap, absorbed in his newspaper. He reminded me of a sailor who'd come ashore, but he couldn't have been – there wasn't any shore within 300 miles of us. I needed to focus.

'What's going on with that?' Phil was asking.

'The REE role?'

'Yeah.'

'We're trying to land her.'

'The one you mentioned? The looker?'

'Yes, Kate Novakovich. There was a guy on the debrief call from Maryland. Deep voice. Running the meeting pretty much. Couldn't tell who he was.'

Phil thought for a moment. 'Could have been any number of people. Why didn't you check the meeting invite?'

'We moved the debrief forward at the last minute. The invitation wasn't updated.'

'You didn't think to do a round of introductions?'

'I arrived late. Listen – the chat on the call was about this merger with Xanant . . .'

'What about it?'

I had Phil's full attention now.

'It looks like it's going ahead,' I said, 'but they need Kate Novakovich – or someone like her – to show that they have business out east. There were lots of references to "showing the value" there.'

'Certainly sounds like the merger's on,' Phil said approvingly.

'But how does it really help, having one extra person on the payroll in Moscow? What does that show?'

'Shows our intent,' Phil said, attacking his pint, froth appearing on his upper lip. 'Depending how well we tell the story . . . Doesn't the job description have her building out a team, pronto?'

'It does.'

'*Et voilà*,' he said in his nasal, Estuary English.

But it only explained so much. Who was the man with her, and what had happened on Saturday night?

'What does it all mean?' I wondered aloud.

As I said it, I noticed my BlackBerry blinking again. The emails never let up. This time, though, it was a text from Claire. I didn't have the energy to open it.

'Means a lot of people are about to make shitloads of money. Less so you, mate.' Phil clinked my glass.

He was talking about my relative lack of stock options.

'Anyway, I'm going to be out of the country for a couple of weeks,' he said. 'Somewhere warm.'

'I see.'

'The Caymans, actually.'

'For work?'

'Unused vacation time,' he said, slipping into an American accent.

'What will you do out there?'

His brow furrowed. 'Dunno, haven't really thought about it. Same as here, probably.'

'Watching the footy?'

He shrugged, then craned his head to see the TV screen. But there was no football on tonight, just the BBC World News. The Russian elections: the robust figure of Igor Strokan, the Kremlin's new Tsar-like leader, immobile at the head of a meeting of oligarchs – library footage establishing his 'power vertical' status in Moscow. The camera cut to the younger, campaigning figure of Dimitri Karaulov, striding through the streets, stopping here and there to shake hands with voters, his sleeves literally rolled up, projecting hope and justice.

The sailor (who wasn't a sailor) was staring at the TV, too.

'Would you mind looking out for the Maserati?'

'Seriously?' I turned to Phil. Suddenly the autobahn beckoned, just the other side of the border . . .

'Not driving it, you twat! Just making sure it's OK – that someone hasn't slashed its tyres or something.'

'What a generous offer . . . Tyre-slashing, in Luxembourg?'

'Trust, but verify,' and he winked.

It was the second time I'd heard that

By seven I was back at my apartment building. I slowed as I approached, looking up at the opposite side of Avenue de la Liberté.

I looked back at my own building and then at the one opposite again. The day before, the police had visited Mme Doriot, following up on the complaint about me rescuing Mischa from the roof. The complainant must live in the top apartment; it was the only one with a view over the wall-head gutter of my building. What else might he or she have seen? Something on Saturday night as well, perhaps? My shutters had been closed the following morning, but they wouldn't have been when I got back there with my female companion.

I crossed the street and rang the top bell of the opposite building. There was no response, so I tried the concierge's office.

'*Oui*?' a soft, male voice said.

'Do you speak English?'

'Yes, a little.'

'I need to talk to the occupant of the top-floor apartment.'

'Who is this?'

'I live opposite. Could I come in?' I didn't want to have this conversation in the street.

The door clicked open and I entered a large lobby. As the light switched on, I saw that it was stripped bare. There was plastic sheeting on the floor, bearing the logo *Daleiden*.

A young man appeared, fresh-faced and clear-eyed. He had an entrepreneurial air about him. The property developer, perhaps?

'Could I talk to the person in the top apartment?'

'It is empty. The building is being renovated.'

Who had called the police, then?

'No one is living there?' I confirmed.

'No. It is not available for another three months.'

'Perfect, that's when I need another place to rent. Looks like a great location and view. Could I see it?'

He walked away.

'Just for five minutes!' I called after him. 'My company's given me a very generous housing allowance!'

I didn't know whether to wait or not, but thankfully he returned with a set of keys. We took the wide stairs up, which were also bare. Wires sprouted from the walls; the light shone from hanging bulbs and created crazy, latticed shadows through the original iron railings.

We got to the apartment and he opened the door. Inside, it was dark and empty, the smooth parquet floor ponded by pale light; it took him a few seconds to find the light switch.

I made my way over to the windows of the main room, which were blocked by roller blinds. Most buildings in Luxembourg had them and they were usually electrically operated. These blinds had the old straps that you hauled manually; the view opposite revealed itself as I pulled one, the edges of the thick strap burning my hands.

I was looking directly across into my apartment. My hunch had been right: this was the only apartment that could see over the wall head and into my place. The apartment below this one would not have the right angle.

'No one has been here?' I looked around. It was an empty shell; there was no evidence of inhabitation, temporary or otherwise.

'No,' he said quizzically.

So who had called the police? On one side of this building was a street corner and, beyond that, the enormous former headquarters of the ARBED steel conglomerate. On the other side was another apartment building. Maybe that one, then; maybe it had been the people living there. But as I looked back at my apartment, I realised that they couldn't have seen in, which was what I cared about most.

Suddenly my mind went to the open skylight that Mischa had escaped through. Was it me that the witness had seen out there on the roof, or someone else? Someone opening that skylight? Anyone's suspicion would rightfully be aroused by somebody forcing open a window on a roof.

As I thought about that, my eyes tracked down.

In the apartment below mine, I could see the harsh, blue flicker of a TV.

Below that, a woman was walking around her apartment in what appeared to be high heels, from the way she wobbled; it looked like she was trying them on for size.

At the bottom, I caught the main door opening and Mme Doriot appearing with Mischa, the cause of this whole diversion.

I watched them waiting to cross the street.

Then I saw a figure with a luminous head. Blonde. Beside her was a large car, nosed into the side street, a pall of exhaust fumes lit red by the high rear lights. A Range Rover, possibly, or it could have been a people carrier – a taxi waiting?

I looked at the woman again and felt a stab of recognition: Kate.

'I'll let you know. Gotta go,' I told the guy, and ran out

down the stairs, all four flights. I slid on the plastic sheeting in the lobby and almost lost my footing, then flung open the front door; dodging a buzzing scooter, I ran into the avenue and had to wait for a bus to pass – only to find the car and the woman gone.

'Nick!' a voice called.

It was Claire.

Where Now?

Claire threw her arms round me. She was crying, her body limp.

I felt a chill pass through me at the thought that she'd flown all the way over here, but for now I simply held her, one hand pressed between her slim shoulder blades, feeling the fine, damp cashmere of her coat mould to her back. Claire was a paradox through and through: a champion chess player at university, and batshit crazy.

She wriggled free. 'Why have you been ignoring me?'

Her eyes looked fiercely into mine, pooled with tears that glistened in the streetlights. Though I'd known her intimately for over a year, I'd never got the measure of her, or that searching gaze.

'Work's been busy,' I replied.

The work that she'd encouraged me to do. A tear leaked down one cheek. By any standards she was an attractive woman, with a softly rounded face and dimpled chin. Her accent was cut-glass English.

Her teeth were chattering. 'Where to?' She looked right and left. The freezing rain had stopped, but it was still very cold.

'You'd better come in,' I said.

There was a bag by her feet. Just an overnight one – which

was something. I recognised it as the Hermès number that I'd bought her several months back. An entire internship's pay at the temp recruiting firm she'd plugged me into soon after we'd met.

'Maybe we should get a drink first,' she said. 'Your local, the Rose –'

'No,' I shook my head, 'I've just come from there.'

I'd left Phil there with his BlackBerry. I didn't want to run into him or have to explain the situation to Linette.

Claire looked warily at the entrance to my building.

'OK,' she said.

I picked up her bag and led the way.

As we crossed the lobby, she held back – God knows why – but caught up with me as the lift arrived.

We ascended slowly, in silence, my feeling of unease rising. What was her news? Why had she flown over, out of the blue?

I opened my door and turned on the lights. The apartment felt dimmer, gloomier than usual.

'Come in,' I said and turned to her.

She was looking around in confusion, her eyes narrowing. Or perhaps it was embarrassment? Certainly this wasn't the time to become angry with her.

I set down the Hermès bag. 'Can I get you a drink?'

'Yes,' she said, peeling off her coat and laying it over the hall chair. She unzipped her boots and padded through to the living room, sitting down on the black leather sofa. 'A whisky. Do you have any of that Cragganmore left?'

I did, as I discovered after looking in my cupboard: an

unopened bottle of it. I broke the seal and poured her one, then poured another for myself.

'Here,' I said.

She raised the tumbler to her mouth and took a glug.

I sat down in the chair opposite.

'This is unexpected,' I said from behind my whisky glass.

She'd rearranged herself horizontally. She was wearing a faded pair of tight jeans that did nothing to hide her shapely legs, and I felt a familiar and unwelcome pang of desire for her. I couldn't get the last time out of my head – the break-up sex a week or so before; the way she'd thrown her head back, baring her pale neck in abandon.

She took a sip, which turned into another glug.

'Would you like to explain what's going on?' I asked.

'Could we have some music on? It's so quiet in here.'

I sighed and didn't move.

'Do you remember that night we met at that leadership in sport conference, at the bar . . . and what you said to me after a few drinks? You remember? You were wearing that stupid red scarf that you just wouldn't take off.'

Yes, I remembered the stupid red scarf. She would never let me forget it.

'And you asked me, in that accent of yours, about my dad, what he did for a living.'

I remembered all right, how upset she'd become. But this was new, this reminding me of my northern accent . . .

'And I –' She looked at me accusingly. '*What?*'

'Claire. Where are we going with this?'

She ran a finger lazily round the rim of her tumbler. Or rather, attempted to: her hand was trembling.

I stared up at the ceiling.

And there I saw a down lighter with a dead bulb. A little wire was protruding, ever so slightly, from the housing.

Had Mme Doriot entered the apartment again? But she wouldn't have messed with a light bulb. Nor would M. Doriot. I felt a chill pass through me.

'What's up?' Claire said. 'What did I say?'

I looked back at her. 'Nothing.'

She was sitting up now, her stockinged feet on the floor.

'*Nothing*? You don't think anything I have to say is even worth *listening to* any more?' She screwed up her face, incredulous.

'Jesus *Christ!*' I smacked my tumbler down on the low glass table beside me, almost breaking both.

But fear lay behind my flash of anger; instinctively I looked up to the ceiling again. The dead light bulb was recessed. Was there a camera lens in place of the bulb?

'Why do you keep rolling your eyes?' she asked, her own leaking tears again. I stood up. The force of my action surprised me; it was some kind of fight-or-flight reflex. I strode over to Claire, catching her sudden look of fear, and sat down beside her, wrapping my arm around her slender shoulders.

'Maybe we should go out for that drink after all,' I said quietly.

'Why?' She began sobbing again.

We'd been here often, in the same, hopeless place. But the urgency of the required solution was new. I needed to get us both out of here. I knew I was in danger, Claire too.

'Didn't you say you wanted to go to the Rose and Crown?'

She buried her head in my shoulder and I smelled the floral scent of her mussed hair; the golden strands danced with static.

The whole room felt charged.

'Claire,' I said softly, or tried to; I could hear the edge in my voice.

'I don't want to go back into the cold,' she said, her palm travelling up the outside of my hip to my lower ribs. It paused there, fingers splayed as if deciding whether to shove me away or not. Her lips rose and met mine, moist with Cragganmore.

I drew back, our eyes meeting.

There was something achingly vulnerable about Claire's face, which was almost Slavic in its soft roundness.

She pulled her sweater off crosswise over her head: underneath, there was just a black balconette bra pushing her breasts up, her hardened nipples pressing through.

'What?' she said, po-faced. So proper.

So upper-middle-class English.

I kissed her hard, causing her to inhale sharply, her stomach sucking in, her chest pressing up and squashing against mine.

'Here,' I said, unlocking my lips from hers. Then I led her by the hand towards the bedroom – away from that dead light in the living room ceiling.

'You're hurting me!'

I was on top of her, a film of sweat forming between our skin surfaces in the darkness.

'Stop!'

I did. I could feel our chests thumping out of sync. She forced a hand in between us, in an attempt to roll me off.

'*Oww*,' Claire was saying, squashing her thighs together, rolling and wriggling dramatically.

I sat up on my knees, straddling her.

'I didn't ask for rough. What's wrong with you?'

'Sorry,' I said, looking askance.

The shutters were still open, just as I'd left them that morning. The apartment opposite was in darkness as before.

I ran a hand over my head and let it rest at the back of my damp neck, catching the musky smell of my underarm, trying to reorient myself.

Claire was lying still now. She puffed her fringe away from her eyes.

'Just be gentle,' she said, '. . .to begin with.'

I couldn't see her face that well in the darkness. I could only really make out her head, framed by the white pillow. The pale pools of her breasts, too, and the dark, hard buds of her nipples.

'Hold on,' I said, climbing off her.

'Huh?' She pushed herself up on an elbow.

'I need to . . . take a piss.'

'Well, remember to take the condom off,' she said, flopping back down onto the pillow with an angry sigh.

I shut the bathroom door behind me and turned on the light, looking in the mirror. I needed to see myself again: to remind myself of who I was. I know that sounds crazy, but I really was beginning to wonder. Looking into my grey eyes, I saw that my irises had sharpened, pulsing into little coronas with each heartbeat.

I opened the cabinet and rummaged around for a lithium pill. Tubes of toothpaste and shaving balm spilled out. It's not that I'm schizophrenic or bipolar, but I have this family history that I need to guard against. Some rogue gene from my dad's side, apparently. Extreme moments of stress and provocation bring it on. Like one time at the Blackburn End: I wasn't even fighting on the terraces that day, but I was one of the first ones the police got hold of and dragged away, and at that point I didn't make things easy on myself, as the judge later ruled.

It amazed me that the companies I'd worked for hadn't background-checked *me* – especially my current employer.

I swallowed the old-fashioned looking pill – a little cylinder, half-orange, half-yellow – dipping my mouth beneath the tap.

Those troubles dated back to well before I met Claire. I was struck by the old adage that you can spend years with another person yet never know them, their thoughts and secrets. I closed the mirrored door again; my eyes already looked calmer, the irises subdued.

When I got back to bed Claire was on her side, checking her phone, her face bathed in the pale-white light of the screen.

'Everything OK?' I asked. It reminded me that I needed to check mine, see what was going on with Kate.

'Yes,' she said, and I lay down under the covers, allowing her to rest her head on my chest, her chin on her interlaced fingers. 'You?'

'Fine.'

'Nick . . .' She was about to confess something.

I canted my head towards her, feeling the remnants of my erection die. Her head was silhouetted against the window.

'How's work?' she asked.

I laughed at the incongruity of the question.

'*What?*' she protested. 'You seem so busy all the time! What's going on?'

'Oh . . . recruitment. You know.'

She did. She worked in it.

She gave up her questioning and got to the point. 'You asked what news I had.'

I waited.

Her lips trembled. 'There are some things going on that I need to tell you about.'

I was torn. Part of me feared the apartment was bugged; part of me just needed to hear. But instead of Claire's soft voice, there was a sharp rap at the front door: someone was knocking hard, and it wasn't Mme Doriot.

'Hold on.' I got up and pulled on my trousers, shirt and slip-ons.

I walked down the hallway, fumbling with my shirt buttons, my limbs tensing. The spyhole didn't have a fish-eye lens; whoever was the other side of the door was standing to one side.

'Who is it?' I called out.

I could hear mumbling, and Claire saying from the bedroom, 'What's going on?'

'Who the fuck is it?' I said, feeling my fists clench. I wished I hadn't taken that lithium pill now.

'Nick!' Claire had appeared at the bedroom door.

'Get dressed, then go out onto the roof,' I hissed to her. 'There's a wall-head gutter –'

'The hell's going on?' she shrieked, as the door came towards me, the frame splintering and shattering. Light appeared round three edges as if in a vision; the lock flew apart, the door collapsed in on me and I saw stars. I was staggering backwards, a dull ringing in my ears.

'Claire!' I yelled, my voice coming as if from underwater. There was a murky light in front of me and blurry figures were swimming forward. A large hand clasped one of my upper arms tightly. With my free arm I swung a wild punch, my whole body behind it, and felt the knuckles collide with something that crunched; I followed through and the world swivelled and tilted as I fell, the door coming to meet me again, this time rising up with the floor.

Pfaffenthal

A tangy, red darkness.

A metallic taste: blood in my mouth.

I was on the back seat of a moving vehicle, rocking, the central markings of a road striping along in the yellow light of the headlamps. My head lolling heavily, one side to the other.

The headlamps lit up the white stripes around the base of trees, a flashing curve of them around a lazy bend in the road. I fell over, cord cutting into my wrists, bound behind me. Another thump as my head hit something, or something hit it . . . then darkness.

I couldn't move. My mouth was woolly and dry. Above me stood tall figures. Two or three.

No, two.

One leaned down. I could feel my eyelid yanked up. A blinding light made me shrink back. A searing pain in the kidneys, where I must have been kicked. More darkness.

Darkness.

'Nick Thorneycroft,' a foreign voice said. Female, older . . . Russian, I was pretty sure. Those *r*'s. I couldn't see her. I tried, but my eyes were too swollen.

'Are you Nick Thorneycroft?' the voice persisted.

I nodded.

'Good.'

I waited, taking stock of the aches and pains in every limb.

'We just have some questions for you, Nick. That's all.' She paused. 'Just questions.'

'Where's Claire?' My voice was muffled.

'We want to talk about Yekaterina. You do know Yekaterina, don't you?'

Kate – what had become of Kate?

'Could you confirm for us that you know Yekaterina Novakovich by nodding your head – just so that we don't have to hurt you again?'

I nodded.

A light shone brighter through my swollen eyelids. I tried to turn away, but a hand held my face there.

'Good. Now, why are you trying so hard to recruit her?'

Who were these people? The competitor company, Xanant? I'd heard about dirty tricks in business before, but this? Whatever was going on, this was a different game altogether.

'To build up our REE business . . .'

'REE?'

'Russia and Eastern Europe.'

'All this effort and haste, just to have her build another business line for you?'

'Who are you?'

Another excruciating pain in the kidneys; it rolled through every part of me. I keeled over.

'We ask the questions, Nick. It's very simple. Very, very simple. Why are you making this difficult?'

I was hauled upright onto my aching kneecaps. Bare concrete beneath me, it felt like.

'Why are you trying to recruit her?' A sharpness had entered her voice.

'Because I've been asked to.'

'By who?'

'My boss.'

'Which one?'

I thought of Charlotte, in that conference room, staring out into the darkness. 'I can't tell you.'

More all-enveloping pain and then darkness, and this time it lasted a while.

Another person, another voice: avuncular this time. I was blindfolded. It was funny; through the blottings and shards of pain, I thought of M. Doriot in his stripy pyjamas.

'You have only recently joined the company, Nicholas.' A polite cough. 'You join, and within a few short months you try to recruit this woman in particular. Why her? We're just curious. You say you were *told* to recruit her.' He gave a little laugh, 'But why? They must have given you a reason!'

'I . . . they asked me to,' I said. 'It's a company. There's a chain of command.'

A thought flickered in the dulled hemispheres of my brain: the Belgian ex-police captain we'd hired to investigate the Benelux candidate. But these people didn't seem like corporate-investigation types. What private investigator smashes in the door of a Luxembourg apartment at night?

'Talk to me about it.'

I heard a chair creak, the man adjusting his weight in it.

'Would you like a sip of water? Here.'

My lips quivered as they sensed the edge of a cup. Cool liquid trickled into my mouth. My sense of taste had gone; it could have been strychnine for all I knew, yet my body craved it.

The cup was withdrawn and I felt the liquid dribbling wastefully down my chin.

'Well?' the voice continued.

What did I owe anyone? I'd been through enough.

'They want to get themselves bought out by another company. They thought if they could recruit Kate – Yekaterina – and show that they had business in Moscow, then . . . they could be . . . They could get more. Money.'

By the end, the effort of speech had turned me monosyllabic. My throat, larynx, chest ached to the core.

'All this effort,' the voice said, 'just so a company can improve its chances of being bought out. Do we believe that?'

He must have been addressing others in the room, or someone elsewhere. He'd leaned forward, I knew, because his voice was closer. 'Let's hope so, Nicholas. Because if not,' he was closer still, 'things are about to get very nasty for you. Very nasty indeed.'

A hand smoothed my hair. That was the most sinister part of all.

'You're sure you're telling us the truth now?'

I was pretty sure I was, but I'd lost track. I hoped to God I didn't betray as much.

A final stinging *whap* across my face and I was back on the ground, out cold.

When I came to, a dark red bar hovered above my head. I was outdoors in pale light.

Birdsong.

I felt a prod to the arm; it was a stick, held by an old man. Glassy-eyed, he looked down at me.

'*Ça va?*' he asked hoarsely.

A car whooshed past. The noise came from nowhere and vanished just as fast.

I propped myself up on the gritty surface of a pavement, aching everywhere.

The dark red bar was the Red Bridge, directly above me. I was in Pfaffenthal, the blue-collar area known mostly for being where people jumped off the bridge. More than a hundred poor souls had done so since it opened, apparently – and I felt like joining them. If Luxembourg was a snow globe, this was the bottom of it – its netherworld.

The old man had lost interest in me. He shuffled away. I picked myself up and stood, taking a moment, bending forward, my hands pressed on my knees.

My numbed hands were grey from the cold, my roughened nails blue-white.

Evidently I'd been dumped on the pavement. I tried not to think any more; my brain felt swollen at the centre.

I knew that it was only a short walk along the Alzette upstream to the office, where a hot shower awaited.

I set off, limping.

Hopefully, it was early enough that I wouldn't run into anyone there. I needed a chance to clean up; my trousers were torn, my shirt was ripped. I kept a spare set of clothes in the drawers of my desk. How would I get through the two inner security doors without my pass, I wondered. Hugging my sides for warmth, I moved as fast as I could, one foot scuffing the rough tarmac.

What about Claire? I needed to call the police – and Mme Doriot too. I picked up the pace, and before long was following a delivery man into the reception area of the office, waiting for him to leave again so I could clamber, agonisingly, over the security turnstile and into the corridor where the showers were.

I slumped to the floor in a cubicle, pulled off my clothes and slapped on the shower, letting the hot water run over me, the grime and dried blood running away in steady rivulets.

Eventually, I scrambled upright, turned off the shower and ventured a look in the mirror.

The man I saw wasn't me. A split lip, eyes blue-black and swollen, abrasions all down my left cheek: I needed to get out of there, before someone saw me. But I also needed clean clothes, which were in my desk drawer.

I found a pair of discarded tracksuit bottoms under the bench in the changing area and salvaged my shirt and slip-ons. There was no clock and I wasn't wearing my watch, but I guessed that it was before seven. Even Charlotte Newbury didn't get in this early.

So imagine my surprise when a Porsche 911 rumbled

past the glass wall in reception and a hand waved: Mike Duchelle's. He veered into a visitor parking space, eased his bulk out of the small sports car, and headed straight towards me before I had a chance to do anything about it. Bulk and agility – that's what it meant to be a former American football player, apparently.

'Hey sport!' He did a double take. 'Were you in a bar fight?'

'I was attacked.'

'Jesus. Where. Here?' He looked round incredulously.

'No, listen, I don't have my pass. We need to call the police. It's about Kate.'

'Kate?' His brow furrowed. 'Katrina? The candidate?'

'Yes, I was taken from my apartment and bundled into the back of a car. Government people: Russian security forces, I'm pretty sure.'

He held up a palm as though administering a benediction, but he was shaking his head.

'Slow down, sport. You're not making sense. The who, now?'

'I can't be sure, but I think it might have been the FSB – the Russian Federal Security forces. They smashed in the door of my place. Who else does that? Then they interrogated me about her: why we were recruiting her, what was going on –'

'You need to slow down and sit down. Here.' He rolled over a chair from behind the reception desk. 'Did you get hit on the head?' He peered into my swollen eyes.

'Yes. But we're wasting time. People are at risk. We need to call –'

'Who's at risk?'

Behind him, a new cobalt-grey Aston Martin Rapide glided into the parking area: Charlotte's. This was unbelievable.

Mike looked over his shoulder.

'Let's not be too hasty,' he said urgently. 'Let's just break this down into manageable components. You were attacked by someone. You've had a bad concussion. It can trigger all kinds of voices in the head. I know. I once had a bad tackle –'

'No,' I said. 'You're not listening to me. These people are fucking serious.'

'This merger is fucking serious,' he hissed. 'And happening! It's coming straight in down the flight path. We can't have the company involved in a police enquiry.'

Charlotte walked in slowly, speaking into her hands-free headset.

'Get yourself cleaned up,' Mike said, leaning in to me. 'Then we need to get the candidate's John Hancock on her employment contract. You hearing me? Nick?'

My eyes met Charlotte's. Hers widened a fraction.

'Hold on,' Charlotte said to whoever was on the phone. 'Let's continue this when I reach my desk. I'll dial back in.'

Mike nodded a greeting to Charlotte and walked away.

'I don't know what kind of night out you've had,' Charlotte said to me, with such nonchalance that I wondered for a second whether I'd been beaten after all or whether this had all just been a bad dream, 'but you'd better be presentable again by Friday night.'

I couldn't think what she meant.

'The Financial Services Ball,' she reminded me.

The biggest social fixture on the finance industry's calendar, for which Charlotte had booked the head table and for some reason assigned me a seat.

'And Nick – let's try to have Yekaterina sitting at our table, too. Not Xanant's.'

Room 550

Before leaving reception, I grabbed hold of the phone behind the desk and tried Claire's mobile, a number I knew by heart.

There was no reply.

I took off through the main doors, noticing pallets of shrink-wrapped furniture stockpiled in the lobby of Building Two.

Maybe Claire had made it out onto the roof and was now somewhere safe.

I made for the apartment. Fifteen minutes later, I'd crossed the Adolphe Bridge and was walking towards a little electronics store on Avenue de la Liberté. It was the kind of shop you might expect to find in a small market town back in England, oblivious to the Internet in its limited range of products, yet it glittered in the strengthening sunlight. Gathered around its window was a group of sharply suited men.

The flashing TV in the shop window was showing scenes of disorder on the streets of some city: black-uniformed security officers, like storm troopers, with layered shoulder protectors – modern-day armour, hauling away the unprotected. There were red flares and tear gas – plumes and curlicues of the stuff.

In the background, I could see the coloured, bulbous spires of Saint Basil's Cathedral. It was Moscow: the presidential elections. The well-dressed men around me were speaking Russian. Probably fund managers on their way to work.

'What's going on?' I asked one of them. He looked me up and down in my torn shirt and tracksuit bottoms, then continued his conversation.

I walked on to my apartment building.

The door of Mme Doriot's was open and I could see her sitting at her table, head in hands, sobbing.

'What happened?' I asked.

'Mischa is gone.'

It was like some Luxemburgish Groundhog Day.

'M. Doriot, too.'

I drew closer. 'M. Doriot?'

'He was taken . . . by those men.' Tears were streaking her foundation. Her watery eyes took in the state of my face. 'What happened to *you*?'

'Have you spoken to the police?'

'Yes,' she said through more sobs, 'and they want to speak with you too, *Nicolas*. And this time, you must speak to them!'

I thought about Mike's admonitions about the police, and then the idea of M. Doriot being subjected to the kind of interrogation I'd just been through. My fists clenched at the needless thuggery of it all.

'I will,' I promised.

I went to my apartment. A locksmith (I assumed) had fitted a temporary door; it looked ugly and flimsy in the formal old door frame. I pushed it open. Inside, the place was just as before, except for a note on the table by the leather sofa:

Nick,
I suppose those were bailiffs? (Didn't I try to warn you about your debts before you left London?)
I decided to go back. We can talk another time.
x C

This was unbelievable. I scrunched up the note. What on earth was up with her? Had she not taken in *anything* that had happened last night? Besides, I'd paid off all my debts. Well, almost. The tax bill was taking a little longer than the others, but –

Who in their right frigging mind could mistake the Russian FSB for debt collectors? Jesus! I threw the balled note into the corner of the room.

The bottle of Cragganmore was still out, so I poured myself a healthy measure and found some aspirin. I wasn't going to go into work today. In fact, I wasn't going to go into work at any point until the swelling had gone down and my Elephant Man face had returned to normal.

I took off the ill-fitting clothes and binned them, then went through to the bathroom, carrying my whisky with me.

The mirror showed me my battered and swollen face again. And in it, I saw the angry features of my father. With dismay, I saw how – as we grow older – we resemble our parents more and more, physically at least.

Fuck. I shuffled back through to the living room to find my BlackBerry.

Nothing from Claire.

Plenty from work. Two hysterical texts from Darrel Casablancas – *Have you heard from Yekaterina?* – in exact duplicate. Terse emails from both Mike and Charlotte.

Nothing from Kate.

I set the blinking phone down, poured another Cragganmore and slumped onto the leather sofa, closing my eyes.

Like a bad dream, the events of the previous night came tumbling back. I shuddered at the memory of the shadowy figures interrogating me.

Then I thought of the storm trooper images on TV.

I stood up again and went over to my desktop computer in the corner of the room. I waited for it to whir and click into life, then went to the web and searched for Russian news.

The BBC website explained the outbreak of violence: *Financial scandal envelops Russian elections. Opposition leader calls for answers on President's offshore wealth . . .*

I found myself walking around my living room in small circles. Was it possible?

Surely not . . .

I pulled up my work address book on my Blackberry and scrolled down, my bruised fingers fumbling, only to recall that Phil had gone to the bloody Cayman Islands. I scrolled back up, found Bjorn Hardwick's number and hit dial.

'Yep,' his flat voice answered.

'Bjorn? It's Nick Thorneycroft here. Do you have a minute?'

'In fact, I have three minutes before my first call.'

'OK, what data does a Vice President at our company have access to?'

He was silent for a second. 'What type of data are we talking about? Could you define your use case?'

Opposition leader Dimitri Karaulov claims President Strokan has almost one trillion US dollars stashed in overseas bank accounts...

'This Head of REE we're trying to recruit.'

'Hm,' he said. 'If I tell you, will you help me fuck her?'

I winced, unsure whether he was joking or not.

'Bjorn, mate. That's not how the dating game works here in the modern age. One night we'll go out on the town, look at your technique. In the meantime, would she have access to offshore payments concerning private, high-net-worth individuals or investment vehicles?'

'Russian ones?'

'Yes.'

'Why do you need to know this?'

... likely located in Switzerland or Luxembourg...

'Just a standard background check. Risk analysis and reduction.' I took a risk myself. 'Charlotte Newbury asked for it.'

'Well, the answer is yes; if she didn't already have that access, she could request it and would likely get it.'

'What if it was a big figure she was asking about?'

'Define "big figure".'

'The President of Russia?'

There was some footage of President Strokan at a news conference (a media privilege not accorded to the opposition leader, apparently). 'Show us the evidence,' a voiceover said in translation, over Strokan's pursed, barely moving lips and beady-eyed glower.

'Data is data,' Bjorn was saying. 'Access is access.'

I was now convinced that Kate was working for the political opposition in Russia (was the man I'd seen her with at the hotel her handler?) and that the FSB knew about it and had come for her. A weariness swept over me as I considered my options: trying to explain things again to Mike and Charlotte, or going to the Luxembourg police – which I needed to do anyway, after the conversation with Mme Doriot . . .

'Hello?' Bjorn was saying.

'I'm still here.' I couldn't think of anything else to ask him. 'That just about covers it, Bjorn. Thank you.'

I ended the call and sat down heavily on the sofa.

My head rolled to one side.

My body must have been craving sleep, because I fell into a deep dream-state . . .

I went looking for Kate at her hotel. Only, when I got there the staff didn't know anything about her. So I persuaded the liveried doorman to take me up to her room. He left me there, alone. She wasn't in the bedroom, but the door to the bathroom was ajar.

I peered in.

Kate was in the bath and immediately saw me, and what must have been my look of surprise: her wet hair lay wreath-like over her breasts; in place of her shapely legs was a great serpent's tail; she splashed and thrashed to cover it up, and I must have been yelling because I woke myself with a start.

I blinked hard. It was already dark outside: I'd been out for hours. My mouth was scratchy dry and I could still taste the Cragganmore.

I poured myself a glass of water this time, took a cool shower and got dressed.

My phone rang as I was leaving the apartment, a withheld number.

'Hello?' I said. Could it be her?

'Nick.'

Charlotte Newbury.

I paused. 'Hi there.' I closed the main door behind me.

'You're not at work.'

'No, not today. I needed to clean myself up, as you probably saw.' I was still aching as I walked down the dark avenue.

'That was this morning. Now it's the afternoon. Are you not feeling better?'

'Somewhat.'

'Where is the candidate?'

'I'm trying to find her.'

A red Ferrari was burbling away at the traffic lights before the bridge. Beside it was a tractor. Each appeared to challenge the other as rightful occupant of the road.

'Others would be more than willing to do your job, Nick.'

I imagined Darrel Casablancas nodding vehemently in the background.

'Tick, tock,' she added.

I felt a flush of anger at having withheld Charlotte's identity from the interrogators and taking even more of a beating for it.

'I'm going to her hotel right now, Charlotte.'

I don't know if she heard me over the traffic noise – the Ferrari screeching away from the green light like a banshee.

She said: 'And don't forget about the FSB.'

The *FSB*?

Wait, was she talking about the Financial Services Ball?

The phone was silent on the other end.

She'd hung up.

At the Hotel Cravat, I approached the swarthy-skinned man at the front desk.

'I came by the other day,' I said, 'about the room with the view and the balcony. I'd like to book it.'

He checked. 'It has become available . . .'

My heart quickened. 'The occupants checked out?'

Had she been taken?

'Yes, it is available,' he repeated.

'Could I see it, make sure I want it?'

'I'm not sure it has been cleaned yet.'

It was after 5 p.m., I was about to remonstrate, but he'd already picked up the phone and was speaking in French.

'Yes, that's fine. Housekeeping finished there earlier,' he said to me.

I cursed myself for not getting here sooner.

'OK, how do we do this? Does someone accompany me up there?'

He looked around. There were no other staff.

'Here.' He handed me the key – an old-fashioned, weighty metal one. It was attached to a little plaque bearing the hotel's name, designed not to be left anywhere by mistake. It must have been in Kate's hands just hours before.

What had happened to her?

'Please do not touch anything in the room.'

'I'll be back in five minutes.'

I made my way over to the main bank of lifts and entered an empty car, hitting the '5' button. The dream came back to me, with Kate in that bath. I thought, too, of the time she'd almost caught me outside room 550.

Standing in front of the door to it, I gave a courteous knock.

No reply, so I turned the key in the lock.

The room occupied a corner of the building; it was more spacious than the one in my dream, with a bed to one side and – on the other – a writing desk and chair. There was another, lower chair.

It could almost qualify as a suite.

I switched on the overhead light. There was a faintly familiar smell, cinnamon-like, of Kate.

But the room was absolutely clean, the covers on the bed perfectly smooth. I walked to the window, where I parted the thin net curtains and opened the doors onto the balcony: traffic sounds rose up from Boulevard FDR and there was a harsh orange light, illuminating the face of the building from below.

I walked back in and opened the door of the bathroom.

No bath. Just a shower, sink, toilet and bidet. I checked inside the cabinet doors: nothing.

I even looked inside the toilet cistern. There was absolutely no evidence of her stay in that room.

Then I tried her mobile phone again. Of course, no response.

I walked back to the balcony and out into the cold bright air. Across the dark void of the Pétrusse Valley stood the old polygonal clock tower of the State Savings Bank. I scanned the skyline, over to the KBL Private Bankers building on Boulevard Royal, lit up a vivid, swimming-pool blue. All the visible landmarks were monuments to money, to Luxembourg's liquidity, its place in the world's financial markets. At one time locals had held up wagons crossing Europe for tolls; now they took a snip of each transaction pulsing virtually through . . .

That is, except for the monument facing me. The war memorial: an obelisk with a golden female on top, forlornly holding a wreath out in front of her as she falls forwards.

There was an ineffable, inestimable beauty about it: the way her flimsy garments clung to her, her thighs bracing for the fall.

I closed the balcony doors and looked around the room once more. The desk, the bedside drawers: all empty.

There had to be something, some clue, some residue of her stay, dammit.

I got down on my hands and knees, feeling the ache, remembering the bare concrete that had pressed into them just hours before.

But the carpet here was soft. There were dust bunnies under the bed.

There was something else, too.

I reached out, patting around with my hand, and encountered spikes. I pulled the object out.

A hairbrush.

I stood up and held it to the light, studying the glistening strands of golden hair.

Back at the front desk, I handed in the key and tried one last ploy.

'I think this room was occupied by an employee of the company I work for. She left this,' and I held up the hairbrush.

The receptionist looked at it blankly, then at me.

'Could you just confirm that Yekaterina Novakovich was staying here and checked out today?'

I looked over my shoulder and saw a man pretending to consult the little tourist cards and brochures at the side of the lobby. He stole a glance my way. Over six foot, dark clothes, flat nose: pure muscle.

'I'm sure you understand the need for confidentiality and discretion,' the receptionist was saying.

'Yeah,' I said, my heart beating faster. 'I do.'

Luxembourg's Landlord

I left the hotel and, instead of turning onto Boulevard FDR, headed up Rue Chimay into the warren of little streets there. I knew the man was following me, about ten paces behind. I now wondered whether I'd been followed before: the businessman tucking into his veal at the Mansfeld, the sailor in the Rose and Crown? If I had been, then this guy had none of his predecessors' subtlety.

I reached for my phone, noting the missed calls and new emails. I dialled Bjorn Hardwick's mobile.

'Hey Nick, I'm on another call –'

'Bjorn, this is an emergency: we're losing the candidate.' It was important not to give him too much time to think, to react. 'Charlotte Newbury wants to know about the transaction report posted to the credit-card account of the hotel she was staying at.'

I turned onto Rue Louvigny; the man followed.

'Nick, I'm not following you. The what, now? You're asking about a hotel's payment-processing records?'

'The Cravat's, yeah. Today: an amount was posted earlier. The room number is 550. That should identify the post.' And the identity of Kate's handler, I hoped.

Bjorn was silent, doing his own processing.

He asked me to explain it all again and I did.

'But that information is confidential to the account –'

'I thought you said that VPs here had access?'

I'd stopped in front of an old-fashioned hat shop, and as I doubled back I almost ran into the guy. He lowered his head and I passed the bill of his cap within inches.

Bjorn was protesting.

'Is Charlotte not a VP?' I interrupted him.

'I don't understand the request.'

'I don't either,' I said, 'but we need to follow through on it. Now.'

I have this theory that, in each of us, there is a little daemon – purple-coloured, in my case – who gives the real orders. And the orders, or drivers, come from above or beyond, or who knows where. But once that daemon's come out to play, there's nothing you can do about it. Sure, you can manage it to a degree, try to act different, but it's a losing battle . . .

My daemon was flexing the fingers and knuckles of my free hand.

'Don't we need to get Central Security involved?' Bjorn was saying.

'We do,' I agreed, to humour him. 'That's my next call. But you know how long that can take. The online forms, submissions . . . Charlotte wants it done now.'

'Can she send me an email? I'll email her –'

'No, Bjorn! There's no time for any of that. Just pull the report and call me back. Or email me. Hotel Cravat, room 550, posted today. We need to know whose account.'

He was saying something about process, standard operating procedures . . .

'Bjorn, I gotta go too.'

I hung up.

There was a chance he'd email Charlotte anyway and I began to compose a response in my head in case he did: 'All a big misunderstanding, Bjorn must have misheard . . .' I jogged to the other side of Rue Chimay and into a narrow, enclosed passageway that connected to Place Guillaume via a set of ascending steps. It was finely surfaced in smooth, dark slate.

I turned to the man following me and we almost ran into each other again, only this time I said: 'Are you from around here?' like I was about to ask directions. His eyes widened in surprise.

I chose a roundhouse punch to his temple. My fist connected well and glanced off his nose on the way around. Clearly he hadn't been expecting this either, because he went down hard. Assisted by the gravity of his fall, I got him arranged so that he was sat with his head slumped forward, dark red dribbling down his upper lip.

A well-to-do woman came clacking down the steps in heeled boots and I shrugged my shoulders at her, as if to say: 'What do you do about these people?'

She gave a complicit eye roll; clearly she had places to go.

I jogged up the steps and into airy Place Guillaume. It had been temporarily renamed Wilhelm under the Nazis. Luxembourg had managed its way through that transition, too, remaining remarkably intact. I shook my bruised knuckles out and flexed my fingers.

My phone was ringing. It was a withheld number, but I

guessed it was Bjorn calling back from his office landline.

I was right.

'OK,' he said, 'I got one of my guys to do it. I hope it's good news.'

'Maybe you could share the news; I'll be the judge.'

'It's a house account, belonging to Daleiden.'

'Jacques Daleiden?'

'Yeah.'

I froze. Jacques Daleiden owned most of the Ville Basse, swathes of Belair and Kirchberg – he was the biggest landlord in Luxembourg by a country mile. Up there with the Grand Duke in terms of power wielded. Word was you couldn't get anything done in this town without Daleiden's buy-in.

'Are you sure?' I said.

'Yeah. It was pretty easy to check. It's the same account family as the ones we pay our rent to, apparently.'

Daleiden owned our office building – and the one opposite, too.

'OK,' I said, dumbstruck.

So many questions came to me in that moment. The first was: why would a man like Jacques Daleiden be aligned with the Russian opposition and not with President Strokan's trillion dollars?

'I emailed it all to you.'

I moved into the middle of the large square, glancing at the uneven rooflines, the lit spires of the nearby cathedral. The building features swirled, my stomach churned. There were any number of shadowy balconies, parapets and other vantage points for tracking my every move.

Bjorn had gone. I checked the phone screen. Just a series of hysterical texts from Darrel Casablancas, the last one reading: *This is your last warning!* I hit delete and walked back into the warren of streets I'd just emerged from.

But not via that slate passageway.

I made my way circuitously across town to the Gare area, avoiding the Adolphe Bridge and Avenue de la Liberté altogether. There was an odd, jelly-pink band of sky on the horizon. It had become very cold.

Going to the streets around the train station always felt like stepping behind the stage set of Luxembourg life, into a world of two-by-four wooden props inhabited by transients and misfits: the displaced – or those simply down on their luck.

I checked into a nondescript guest house on Rue de Hollerich, cash only, and assessed my options. There was no way of safely returning to my apartment any more. Phil had gone on holiday. I didn't want to implicate Linette.

I thought of Claire and our few mutual friends in London. I tried to phone her, but there was no reply. Part of me wanted to call her parents, but I couldn't even begin to think how to get hold of her dad, and I didn't feel comfortable tracking down her mum. Claire and I were finally over – of that there was no doubt.

The only option was to go to the police.

I went back out into the cold darkness, walking towards the fortress-like police station at the bottom of Rue de Strasbourg. I passed a brightly lit Chinese grocery store and thought briefly about buying a kitchen knife. The two contradictory impulses ('police' and 'knife purchase') somehow cancelled each other out, and that's when Mike Duchelle's call came in.

'Sport, where are you?'

'We've got a problem,' I said, trying to stay on the front foot, trying to treat this like any other work conversation – everyday stuff at the office. I was still staring at the nine-inch chopping knife in the window of the store.

'You think?'

'The candidate has vanished.'

I looked up and down the street: immigrants and vagrants, milling about in the cold darkness.

'You have too, I'm told.'

Fucking Darrel Casablancas.

'There's something else,' I said, sidestepping his reference to my absence from the office. 'Jacques Daleiden paid her hotel bill.'

'Huh?'

'I went looking for her, at her hotel.'

There was a pause. 'Listen,' he said, changing his voice; I could imagine him taking a more active position in his seat. An alertness prickled up my neck. 'We're thinking it may be good for you to take a break. After that scrape you got into.'

'Oh?'

'Yeah.' Mike's voice had the determined air that had served him so well in deal negotiations.

The chessboard was receding from view. I could no longer see who was moving which piece, and where.

'What about the Financial Services Ball?' I asked. 'Charlotte was keen that I attended.'

Wrong move, to mention Charlotte that way now.

'Don't worry about her,' he said tersely. 'Focus on me. Take a vacation, go somewhere warm.'

'How long for?'

'A month. Maybe two.'

I sensed that, behind it all, Mike still had my back. 'OK,' I said, suddenly wondering whether there would be a company to come back to or whether the merger would already have happened.

'But could I ask a favour?' I said.

'You can ask.'

'Phil Scarrow mentioned that you worked on the Ducal Casino account before. Could you make me an introduction there?'

Ducal Casino

I waited for Mike's email, remaining in my tiny room at the guesthouse on Rue de Hollerich, driving myself mad with questions. The miniscule TV bolted onto the wall showed a permanent snowstorm of interference. But through the blizzard came news from Russia: postponed elections, tanks on the streets of Moscow, martial law instituted by President Strokan.

I knew I needed to leave town. The train station was right there, around the corner. No need for a passport even.

Yet I also had to know what had become of Kate. For reasons I couldn't entirely fathom, she was all that mattered now. I had to confirm that she was the one who'd put me to sleep and started all this madness.

My frustration and curiosity grew by the hour.

There were two paths I could take. One was to Jacques Daleiden. Though it was a city veiled in discretion and secrecy, it was still a small place: it shouldn't be too difficult to find out where he lived or worked. The ex-sportswriter in me was up for that challenge. Mme Doriot would probably know, if I could just get to her without endangering either of us further.

The other path was to Ducal Casino and its CCTV

system. That would surely bring confirmation and closure, if I could just get access to it.

A small mirror above the bathroom sink showed that my facial swelling was receding. I was still waiting for that email of Mike's.

I checked my earlier emails, and found an old one from Charlotte. And this is where I got lucky – or not, depending how you look at it: I'd neglected to register that the Financial Services Ball was taking place *at* Ducal Casino, on Friday night.

The Casino had clearly been modelled on the one in Monte Carlo, or maybe it was the other way round. Either way, I couldn't help admiring its baroque stonework and bubbling fountains. I'd found a dinner suit at a fancy-dress shop on Rue de Hollerich. No part of the fabric had ever grown; it was scratchy, and not particularly warm either.

Nothing had come back to me from that Saturday night; the circumstances surrounding the Lanson and two club sandwiches were as murky as ever. It struck me as incredible that I'd been allowed in at all, in that state – but of course there was my mystery blonde companion to consider.

A collection of Luxembourg's most expensive cars pulled up and dropped off well-fed, Germanic-looking men – large and confident specimens of their race. It was possible the ducal family would be attending, too – maybe even the Grand Duke himself.

I looked over my shiny shoulders but couldn't see anyone following me. I'd scanned the dark shadows and corners of the square and hadn't noticed anything suspicious. So I paced over to the bright, ornate foyer, not breaking stride as two liveried footmen held open the grand doors.

Of course, a greeter caught me on my way into the main *salle*.

'*Bonsoir, monsieur,*' the svelte lady said, blocking my path.

'I'm on Charlotte Newbury's table,' I said.

She asked for my invitation and I repeated my statement. Charlotte Newbury.

I could see into the *salle*: the roulette and blackjack tables, open for business; flutter, hum, gold and glitter. Beyond was a sea of white dinner tables, the silverware sparkling. The champagne buckets contained a good number of vodka bottles, or maybe I was being overly sensitive to the Russian presence I imagined. Everywhere, large men strained the buttons of their dinner suits and well-dressed women hung on their words.

The svelte lady said something about fetching someone.

I stared upwards with amazement: Roma-looking boys and girls swung from trapezes beneath the gilded ceiling, giving the *salle* a circus-like feel.

A large figure blocked my view.

I had to hand it to Mike. His dinner suit was beautifully tailored to his footballer's physique. It made him look more substantial and yet more agile than ever. He must have dropped some serious coin on it; it reminded me of the way Savile Row suits were originally intended to exhibit horsemens' physiques, as opposed to disguising portly money-managers' bodies – or so Claire had explained to me once, educating me in the ways of her class.

Mike gave me an unexpected bear hug, saying low and urgent in my ear: 'What are you doing here, buddy?'

He released me and looked me in the eye. 'Take that break.'

I looked around his big shoulder. I could see Charlotte in a cool, emerald-green dress, very figure-hugging, a champagne flute in her hand at a slight angle – she was listening intently to a large man in a dinner jacket. Was this the Voice from Maryland? Charlotte laughed, her head dropping back, and in that instant she stole a sideways glance and found me.

For a split second our eyes held, and something was transmitted. Something like *This is only a game, for all of us* – or maybe I was imagining it. She returned her radiant attention to her conversation partner.

There was no sign of Kate.

I said to Mike: 'I *am* heading out. But I need that introduction first.'

'The what, now?' He leaned in, his eyes narrowing with a hint of menace.

'Here,' I said. 'And now. I need to talk to the Head of Security. Do that one thing, and I'm gone.'

He appraised me in my nylon fancy-dress-shop suit. 'Why would I do that?'

'Because you said you would.'

He nodded slowly. A deal's a deal. 'But why the Head of Security?'

I explained to him what had happened that night – everything except my almost-certain knowledge that the woman was Kate, and that I just needed to confirm as much, and then I could fuck off forever from the Russian traitoress.

'Mr Thorneycroft,' Charlotte said, having sidled up alongside Mike. She looked down at my suit.

I thought about saying something to her, but the words didn't quite arrive and so Mike filled the void, murmuring something into Charlotte's ear.

She gave a brief nod.

'OK, sport. Your wish is granted,' he said.

It was the first time I'd heard them agree about anything.

Mike led the way. I exchanged a parting glance with Charlotte, and the next time I looked she'd vanished back into the suited crowd.

We arrived at a room on the far side of the building, functional and nondescript. It had the musty smell of paper and bureaucracy, like a government office building. A hollow-cheeked man in a black suit greeted us.

Mike turned to me. 'This is Monsieur Molling, the casino's Head of Security. He'll give you what you need.'

I was starting to get an uneasy feeling – like this was all *too* easy.

Mike extended his bear's paw of a hand. 'So long, sport.'

I shook it apprehensively.

'Good luck,' he said over his shoulder as he left.

'*Venez,*' Molling said, leading me into exactly the kind of space you'd expect the CCTV room of a casino to look like: banks of little TV screens in the semi-darkness, and a man sitting, silhouetted, watching.

Molling went to the back of the room, disappearing altogether into the darkness at one point.

'*C'était quel date?*' came his voice.

'*Samedi dernier. Tard.*'

Last Saturday night, late.

He reappeared with four or five discs.

'*Et voilà.*'

We sat together at a machine. As the first images began to appear on the screen, the watcher lit a cigarette. The acrid smoke in the small space almost made me gag, but I couldn't protest.

I knew that I'd paid for the Lanson and sandwiches at quarter to three in the morning, but there were many bars and payment points in the casino, so it was a question of checking each.

The black-and-white images flickered away in silence.

At one point, Molling got up for coffee and offered me some. I declined, my stomach feeling off from the smoke and the anticipation. The room was astonishingly quiet. Just the hum of the machines and the sound of the watcher occasionally swallowing or moistening his mouth.

I looked over his shoulder at his CCTV screens and fixed on one that showed the sea of people in the main *salle*. I thought that I could make out Mike halfway down the room. He raised a hand to wave at someone; he may as well have been on the far side of the world.

Molling returned, tight-lipped but somewhat perkier, and we kept going.

I'd always imagined that CCTV was the ultimate form of surveillance. But half the images were indistinct; often the camera was not quite at the right angle to be sure of the scene, or the space was too dark; Molling would sigh sharply.

Then we found me. I was moving towards one of the smaller bars off to the side of the main *salle* like some wraith, looking around, asking something of someone, just off camera . . .

My heart pounded.

On screen, the barmaid was waiting for me, her hands pressed into the countertop.

'*C'est bien vous?*' Molling asked.

I nodded. '*Vous pouvez effectuer un zoom arrière?*' My mouth was dry.

He zoomed out as requested and my heart stopped.

The blonde woman who was looking around guardedly was instantly recognisable.

'*Etes-vous OK?*' Molling was saying into my ringing ears, staring at me.

The blonde woman was Claire.

The Bridge

I stumbled out of the casino into the cold night air, my head spinning like a roulette wheel. If someone had wanted to follow me now, they wouldn't have much trouble. I was desperately trying to piece it all together: Claire having been in my apartment, while apparently texting me at the same time – by way of decoy? Claire going through my cabinets, surely knowing about the lithium pills after all, and everything else about me . . . These guilty secrets I thought I was harbouring, when all along she'd been the one living the lie?

Why, Claire Elkin, after the time we'd spent together!

It's funny, her name had always sounded so English to me. Not any more. What with her Slavic-looking features, her chess-playing . . .Was she Russian?

An executive recruiter, recruited by the Russian state?

But what on earth had motivated her? Money?

That didn't sound right, no matter how expensive London living had become.

An outburst of patriotism, perhaps, towards a new Russia? I was shaking my head, walking among the throngs on Rue de la Boucherie, jostled by the Friday-night crowd.

What had she even managed to accomplish? How did it help anyone, Claire getting into my apartment that way?

She'd been at my place before – and after... none of it made sense. For a second, I doubted whether it was even her that I'd seen. Perhaps the CCTV tape had been doctored?

Deep down though, I knew. Little things, like the way she'd hesitated when entering the lobby of my building after she'd shown up unexpectedly on Monday night: she'd been worried about running into M. Doriot again – being recognised as the woman he'd seen on the stairs two nights before. The Doriots had been away the only other time she'd visited me in Luxembourg.

And that must have been the reason why M. Doriot had been taken. The Russian security agents were cleaning up the scene now, comprehensively.

I let myself be swept into Steiler by a party of revellers. It was a haunt of twenty year olds, but it was warm and packed and it was a bar. The young crowd was dancing to Daft Punk. One girl stood on a table, her willowy arms akimbo, eyes glazed, swaying with no correspondence to the music at all, as if on a gentle breeze.

I approached the bar.

'Hi!' a girl with a freckled nose yelled over the music. She almost looked young enough to be my daughter. 'You buying me a drink?'

'No, sorry. I'm just here looking for someone.'

'Yes – me,' she said and laughed, tipping back her head. She sounded faintly Germanic, or hopefully Luxemburgish ... a native. I needed to find Jacques Daleiden now.

'No, really. I'm looking for someone. A friend. Here in Luxembourg. I just can't seem to find his address or phone number.'

'He cannot be much of a friend if you don't know his address or phone number,' she said, placing a steady emphasis on each word, as if she were trying to walk straight, one foot in front of another.

'No. But he has the key that I need.' Or so I hoped.

She tapped another girl on the shoulder and pointed behind the bar: the drink she wanted. I should have asked Molling back at the casino. Maybe I could still go back. The girl turned to me again, handing me a fruit bowl of a pinkish-hued cocktail – Aperol Spritz, the sweet-bitter taste confirmed. The music was suddenly louder; I thanked her and drained half of it.

'What don't you look in Editus?' she was saying.

'In *where*?'

'E-di-*tus*!'

Maybe it was a club.

Her dark, sparkling eyes looked up at me insistently. Challengingly. For a second, I thought of forgetting all about Daleiden and going after her.

'The phone book!' she yelled.

Jesus, only in Luxembourg. Would the town's biggest landlord really be listed right there, in a physical phone book?

It was possible. Anything was possible now.

I found my way to the end of the bar and caught the attention of the barmaid, who was in the middle of taking payment for a disorderly round of shots. The music was even louder here.

'Hey, you got an Editus?' I shouted.

'A what?' She cupped her ear.

'Phone book!'

She turned to an older guy, who appeared to be the owner. At first I thought they were ignoring me. But then the guy reached back and returned with a slim book that had green, slinky springs spiralling across the front. He handed it, flapping, to me.

'Bring it back!'

I took it down the little stairs towards the toilets, into a cramped, stone-arched corridor where there was a ceiling light, and flipped through to D. *Daleiden, Jacques. Montée de Clausen*.

I blinked hard at the pervasive sense of unreality.

The address was just down the hill.

I punched Daleiden's phone number into my BlackBerry and hit save. Then I went back up the stairs, waiting briefly for a guy stumbling down the other way, and returned the Editus to the barmaid.

This time, the cold air outside was a balm. I tried Daleiden's number. There was no reply.

I descended Rue Sigefroi, stopping at the Bock lookout briefly, unsteadily, to take in the frosted twinkle of the Ville Basse, pale under the starry, clear sky. The Alzette roared faintly beneath.

I used the opportunity to look around, at the brightly lit street intersection behind me in particular. A young couple was leaning into each other for balance. There was no one suspicious.

It was madness to go calling on the man this late, but what else was to be done?

I made my way down the hill. I had a vague idea which house it was: one of the large residences off to the right; I'd passed them enough times on my way to work, registering their scale and prime position, looking down as they did over the valley. Charlotte, Mike and the rest of us must have looked up at them a thousand times through our office windows.

I could smell wood smoke – that piquant kind that you tend to find in small French towns and villages. The stone wall and gate didn't offer much by way of security. Again, I looked up and down the street.

The gate pushed open easily enough and led into a dark courtyard, which the house was wrapped around. Beside the front entrance steps sat a low, pale Citroën saloon from the Seventies. No security lights came on. My ears were still ringing from the noise levels in Steiler, and at first I didn't hear the chinking of the dog's lead and its fast breathing. But the black Labrador emerging from the darkness was entirely friendly, unthreatening. It barked just once as I patted its head.

That's when a light came on above the front door.

The old man who appeared wore rustic garb – a waistcoat and kerchief. He looked like a groundsman.

'*Je cherche Monsieur Daleiden*,' I said. '*Quelque chose s'est passé.*'

Something had indeed happened.

'*Et qui êtes-vous?*' he asked, surprised. '*Journaliste?*'

Not a bad guess, given my past. '*Dites-lui: un ami de Kate Novakovich.*' Tell him that I'm a friend of Kate Novakovich.

He appraised me for another second, then looked at

the black Lab, which was quite calm. He bent down and encouraged the dog towards him.

'*Vous êtes anglais?*'

'Yes,' I replied. 'Is Monsieur Daleiden here?'

He gestured for me to enter.

The house appeared smaller, more intimate, on the inside. Dark-wooden stairs ran up from the lobby space. The newel post was carved into a fox's head. The walls were panelled in dark wood, too, giving the place the feel of a hunting lodge.

He led me through to a room at the back with a smouldering fireplace. The Lab padded after us, its tongue lolling.

Through the window I could see the dark sweep of the valley and the woodsman's cottage that I'd noticed from the office; it was at the end of Daleiden's garden.

'Is Monsieur Daleiden in?' I asked again.

'I am Monsieur Daleiden.'

I fought to hide my surprise: *this* man owned swathes of Luxembourg?

'My name's Nick,' I managed. 'Nick Thorneycroft. I work for one of the buildings down there in the valley that you own.'

He held my eyes for a second with his watery blue stare.

'I'm a headhunter. We were trying to recruit Kate Novakovich. Then she disappeared, and I found out that you settled her bill at the hotel she was staying at. Our company handles the payments processing for the Hotel Cravat.'

'Take a seat,' he said, finally.

I sat in a leather armchair, noticing that the fire grate featured little metal foxes too. What was it with that motif? Something about the house being burrowed into the hillside?

'You want to know where Yekaterina is,' he confirmed, sitting in the armchair opposite.

He must have been in his seventies, or older, maybe. There was an old floor lamp behind him, keeping him partially in shadow.

'How much danger is she in?' I said.

He tamped some tobacco down in a pipe, then lit it, sending the spent match spiralling into the fireplace.

'It's not clear.'

He'd disappeared behind a shroud of pipe smoke.

I saw now that foxes were everywhere: on the wallpaper, the handle of the cane leaning against his chair . . . The smoke parted so that I could at least see his eyes. 'What is it that you really want to know?' he asked.

It was like a throwback to the interrogation.

I leaned forward. 'Please. Where's she gone?'

'Hm,' he puffed, eclipsing himself with smoke once more.

'Did Claire have a hand in her disappearance?' I pressed.

'Who's Claire?'

'Claire Elkin.'

'Elkin's daughter.'

'You know him? Them?'

Was Claire's dad in this Russian dissident circle of theirs as well?

Daleiden had retreated into silence.

Was that what lay behind Claire's actions? Had she acted to spite her dad? If he *was* a dissident, did she have to be the opposite?

I sat back and recalled asking Claire about her dad once – the short shrift she'd given me, the striking sense that something had gone very wrong there. But could a child's enmity towards a parent take things *this* far?

'What is it with all the foxes?' I blurted out.

The corners of Daleiden's mouth pulled up into a smile. He sat his pipe down, as though deciding where to begin.

'During the war, they called me "Le Renard". The fox. The country was overrun by the Germans, as you may know.' He paused. 'And they adopted a strategy of total absorption. Young men, like you, were conscripted into the Wehrmacht. If they didn't comply, their wives and families were made to suffer. I had to do something about it.' He gave a shrug, his shoulders surprisingly agile. 'Have you never felt the same urge?'

I ignored his odd question. Lots of older men in this part of the world claimed Resistance records after the fact, I knew.

But somehow, Daleiden's words rang true. My inbuilt bullshit detector, honed over all those interviews – as a journalist – confirmed as much. The tuning fork in my chest was ringing clearly now.

'But why the fox?' I asked.

'Because I helped those people to escape. Into the tunnels under the football stadium; into lots of places,' he indicated with a sweep of his hand.

I'd heard something about this, too; how, when they

rebuilt the stadium on the Route d'Arlon, they'd found all these secret chambers . . .

'With certain tyrannical leaders,' Daleiden continued, 'be they wartime dictators, or modern Russian presidents: you cannot oppose that form of power directly. You can only wait for it to weaken – wait for nature to take its course.'

'You helped Kate escape?'

'She needed assistance.'

'She surely had assistance, from the Russian opposition.' My voice rose. 'That's who she was working for, right? Dimitri Karaulov. She was trying to get the job at my company to access the payment records of President Strokan's offshore wealth. To prove that he has a trillion stashed away, or whatever the loot's now worth?'

Daleiden merely picked up his pipe again.

What drove this old man? The quest for a certain kind of equilibrium – for this town of his, precariously perched in its peculiarly European way? Despite providing an office building to an acquisitive Russian state-payments concern, and relieving this Xanant behemoth of substantial rent payments in exchange, Jacques Daleiden's real fight was to keep the Russians *in check*, I now saw. Just like that wily young man, Le Renard, seventy years before . . .

For could anyone have been truly effective in the wartime Resistance there, without some measure of collaboration, of double-agency?

'It was important to get her out of here,' he said simply.

It occurred to me that he hadn't offered me a drink. Hadn't delayed my onward journey –

'Where *is* Kate?' I asked, this time determined.

He looked at the inside of his wrist, an old timepiece there.

'On her way to the station, for a night train to London.'

I stood.

'I wouldn't attempt to follow her,' he said. 'You won't catch her.'

Again, his choice of words struck me as odd. 'We'll see about that,' I said. 'And by the way, if you're so good at saving people, maybe you could help out a certain Monsieur Doriot.'

I gave him the address – my old one, on Avenue de la Liberté.

Running back up it, the hill felt steeper than before. I thought about the old man between ragged breaths: how he'd pulled Kate away from my company, the Russian opposition, her handler there, and now even the Russian state – outfoxing them all. I ran back past Steiler, cutting through Place Guillaume to Boulevard FDR and the Hotel Cravat, the cold air searing my lungs.

My thoughts kept returning to Claire, and what she'd sought to accomplish.

There was a figure moving hurriedly onto the bridge, silhouetted distantly in the gathering mist.

How did drugging me help her or the Russians? How could she expect not to be found out, once I'd retraced my steps to Zin Zen and Ducal Casino? I was panting, unused to running this fast. The figure bounced with my movement and then her head turned shiny, luminous.

'Kate?' I wheezed.

She kept walking.

'Kate!'

I stopped, resting my palms on my knees, burning up. Sweat dripping beneath the collar of my nylon suit.

She'd stopped too, but didn't turn. Breathing hard, I walked up to her as she stood in the middle of the bridge, her feet frozen in position beneath her long coat. Just a few minutes down the street was the train station, and its illuminated clock tower, but you couldn't see any of that now – not in this mist.

Then she turned to face me, her eyes lighting up the void-like space.

'What are you doing?' I said, breathless.

She cocked her hip slightly, just like she had the first time I'd set eyes on her. Still, she didn't speak.

'Let's just talk about this,' I said.

I felt tears sting my eyes, thinking of everything that might have been there in Luxembourg – which could never be, not now.

'About what?' she said finally.

'I know what's taken place. About the role of Claire Elkin; about you helping the Russian opposition to reveal Strokan's offshore wealth, about –'

'Never mind that, and them. It was you, Nicholas. *You* were our way in,' she said accusingly. 'You were meant to help get me inside that company, and now . . .'

'What?'

'I need a way *out*.'

She looked away, at the darkness of the valley.

'Just tell me one thing: what exactly did Claire do?'

Kate shook her head in exasperation.

'I don't know who exactly you're talking about. But the tactics that the FSB uses are well known: they mean to unsettle, leave you paranoid, make you suspicions . . . of me! Just like you became.'

She turned back to face me, eyes ablaze.

'But it's all over now; Daleiden is helping you get away!'

A sharp exhale of incredulity. 'Do you see him anywhere nearby? You don't win against a man like Strokan,' she cried. 'Not with his foreign network of interests and supporters. You know that by now!'

Her gaze moved around my face, my remaining facial bruising – or perhaps she was taking in my features for the last time.

My BlackBerry sounded the arrival of a text. I pulled it out, the display creating a little globe of light in the mist.

Claire's text came rapid fire, in three parts:

I'm so very sorry. I tried to tell you everything
several times. I wanted so badly for you to know
I love you

I bowed my head. 'Kate,' I started, then stopped.

A shout echoed through the mist simultaneously. 'Yekaterina!'

'It's OK,' I said hurriedly. 'Strokan's already won; he's regained full control of the situation. He's got his tanks out on the streets of Moscow!'

'He has great powers,' she corrected me, 'and great challenges, too.'

'But you're heading to London. He can't threaten you there!'

'You think I can't be found and killed in London? Try telling this to Alexander Litvinenko.'

An image flashed up in my mind of the gaunt dissident, close to his death from Polonium 210 radioactive poisoning – administered over afternoon tea in central London.

'No,' she said loudly, as though for all to hear, 'they've already come for me.'

I turned as the shout repeated itself. '*Ye*katerina!'

I should have realised . . . her not carrying a bag. When I looked back at her, there she was, on the rail of the parapet – swaying.

'*No!*' I yelled.

She was gone again.

I almost went over myself, rushing to try to catch her, the darkness reaching up dizzyingly to claim me too. At the last second I pulled back, my heart leaping into my mouth; I caught a fluttering of fabric and a cry cascading away into the watery depths below.

The cry echoed the length of the dark valley, rising in my ears in pitch and intensity.

Two large men arrived, looked over the parapet and at each other. One shrugged.

Then they disappeared again, into the night.

Coda

It's been more than a year since those tumultuous events. I'm sitting on a bench on Clapham Common in the soft spring sunshine. Dogs bound across the expanse of greenery.

My gaze returns to the newspaper in my lap – the paper I now work for.

There's my article on the first page of the foreign news section, putting a value on the amount of money Russia's President Strokan holds in bank accounts in Luxembourg. It wasn't a trillion, but it wasn't far off. This was the last thing I managed to persuade Bjorn Hardwick to find out for me before handing in my security pass.

It took some time, working up to this exposé. After returning to London, I wrote a few articles in the sports pages, to get my arm back in; I came to focus on the oligarchs behind the Premier League football clubs. What did they hope to gain? A protected place at the heart of the British people, in case the Kremlin turned on them?

I was just happy to be back in the place where I belonged: journalism.

Anastasia is walking among the daffodils and crocus bulbs in her soft black dress. We met through an online dating site. It all happened very quickly: now she's three months pregnant.

Shortly after returning to London, I received Claire's lengthy letter, with its many crossings-out. Hand delivered through my letter box. She mentioned having deliberately *taken risks with her assignment*, having *wanted to confess everything* to me – as she'd tried to do several times, she maintained.

I'd come to see Claire's behaviour as symptomatic of a ruptured parent–child relationship: so often half-in and half-out of situations, as I'd found myself to be, too.

That is, until Anastasia came along. The funny thing is, we don't even talk that much. Although she is starting to teach me Russian.

It just felt right from the start.

She's looking over at the Windmill pub, once a drab old place, now redone to cater to those with money. Like so much of London these days.

'Maybe is good for lunch?' she says, one hip cocked slightly. It's just one of the ways in which she reminds me of Kate.

The bump is starting to show.

'Maybe.'

I fold up the paper. In so doing, I can't help noting another article, about the proposed merger – between Xanant and my old company – tied up in an EU anti-trust investigation. Doubtless Mike, Charlotte and the Voice have some solution up their sleeves, but it can't have been their Plan A. It leaves me thinking about old man Daleiden, up there on the hill in Luxembourg.

In the end, he's managed to recruit me into his cause as well, giving me a certain belief in the kind of country he stands for – keeping foreign aggressors in check. With his assistance, M. Doriot was delivered safely back to his wife. M. Doriot had played dumb with the shadowy people who'd 'questioned' him, he shared later on the phone, shortly after I'd left. I'd finally found the courage to call him and enquire about the body below the bridge.

But there was no body.

The Luxembourg police had searched the area meticulously, Doriot told me, and turned up only a long ladies' overcoat.

Sometimes I fancy I see her face in the crowd, or on an underground train – or even among the joggers and the dog walkers out on the common now. It takes me back to that one moment in the recruitment process, that photo I found of Yekaterina Novakovich, standing beside a set of asymmetric bars, her eyes calm yet determined. The prominent wrist tendons, the chalky-white hands . . .

I can't quite bring myself to go back to Luxembourg, to study the bridge, recall that darkness as she vanished – the distinct possibly that, somehow, she'd managed to grab hold of a ledge below the parapet. Maybe one day I will go back. But not for some time. By which point, the bridge will likely have been rebuilt anyway, renovations to the old structure having been long overdue even before I'd left.

'Are you coming?' Anastasia calls, holding out her hand.

'Sure,' I say, cheerfully enough. 'Just give me a minute.'

Thank you for reading *The Candidate*. Reviews can be tremendously helpful to both authors and other readers. Please consider leaving one for this novella on amazon.co.uk or amazon.com.

To receive occasional updates and offers of free exclusive content, please sign up at danielpembrey.com.

Book Group Reading Questions

1. What role does Luxembourg's location and history play in the story?

2. What was your reaction to the work place depicted at Nick's company?

3. What prevents Claire from being a more knowable character? How did your perception of her change as the story unfolded?

4. Once Nick becomes aware of the danger he's in, why doesn't he go to the police? What impels him to continue to try to solve the mystery himself?

5. Jacques Daleiden, 'Luxembourg's landlord', draws parallels between the regimes of wartime Germany and latter-day Russia: is that valid?

6. By the end of the story, how much has Nick moved on from his experiences in Luxembourg?

NOW OUT

THE HARBOUR MASTER

Maverick cop Henk van der Pol is thinking about retirement when he finds a woman's body in Amsterdam Harbour. His detective instincts take over, even though it's not his case. But Henk's bigger challenge is deciding who his friends are – not to mention a vicious street pimp who is threatening Henk's own family. As his search for the killer of the woman in Amsterdam Harbour takes him into a corrupt world of politics and power, Henk finds himself facing some murky moral choices.

The Harbour Master delivers for Amsterdam what fans of Scandinavian crime fiction have come to love: a fascinating light shone of the dark side of a famously liberal society, combining vivid characterisation with ice-cold suspense.

Available in Kindle edition.

Printed in Great Britain
by Amazon